MYSTERY AT
SARATOGA

Trixie
Belden

Your TRIXIE BELDEN Library

Trixie Belden and the
MYSTERY AT SARATOGA

BY KATHRYN KENNY

Cover by Jack Wacker

GOLDEN PRESS
Western Publishing Company, Inc.
Racine, Wisconsin

CONTENTS

MYSTERY AT
SARATOGA

"Regan's Disappeared!" • 1

TRIXIE, PLEASE COME meet me at the clubhouse right away," Honey Wheeler said urgently.

Even over the telephone, Trixie Belden could tell that her best friend was upset. Honey's voice sounded choked, as if she were struggling to hold back tears.

"What is it, Honey? What's happened?" Trixie demanded.

"Oh, Trixie," Honey wailed, the tears that she'd been holding back finally spilling over, "Regan's disappeared!"

"What!" Trixie gasped. "When? Why? . . ."

"Just meet me at the clubhouse right away, please," Honey begged. "I'll tell you everything I

13

know about it when you get there."

In her haste, Trixie all but threw the receiver back onto its cradle. Calling out, "I'm going to the clubhouse, Moms," she dashed out the door into the hot August sunlight.

Trixie ran along the pathway that led from Crabapple Farm, where she lived with her parents and her brothers. Although she was running practically at full speed, she knew that the pounding of her heart was not altogether due to her exertion.

"Regan's disappeared!" Honey had said. With those two words, the peacefulness of the summer was shattered. Bill Regan—known simply as "Regan" to everyone in Sleepyside-on-the-Hudson— had been hired to take care of the Wheelers' horses long before the Wheelers moved to the Manor House.

When the Wheelers bought the big mansion just west of the old farmhouse where Trixie lived, one of Trixie's fondest dreams—to have a best friend her own age living nearby—had come true.

Then, when she discovered that the Wheelers also had a full-time groom and a full-fledged stable at the Manor House, Trixie felt as if she must be the luckiest girl on earth.

To top it all off, the Wheelers had adopted Jim Frayne, an orphan whom Honey and Trixie had befriended when he ran away from his cruel stepfather, a mean and greedy man named Jonesy.

Jim, Honey, Trixie, and Trixie's two older brothers, Mart and Brian, had all become the best of friends. Together, they had formed a semisecret club called the Bob-Whites of the Glen, in order to organize special events to help worthy causes. The clubhouse to which Trixie was hurrying through the heat of the late afternoon belonged to the Bob-Whites. It had originally been a gatehouse for the Manor House, back before the days of the automobile. The Bob-Whites had discovered it overgrown with weeds and had restored it with hard work and loving care.

It's all been "perfectly perfect," as Honey would say, Trixie thought, half-smiling in spite of herself at her best friend's favorite expression. *I've been so happy since Honey and Jim have been at the Manor House, and I know Honey feels the same way.* Honey had been frail and timid, frightened of her own shadow, when she moved to Sleepyside. But the time she'd spent with "tomboy Trixie" had changed all that. This summer, she was brown as a berry and just as ready for mischief as was her sandy-haired, freckle-faced friend. Having Jim for a brother, after being an only child all her life, had helped, too.

But now. . . . "Regan's disappeared!" Honey's voice echoed in Trixie's mind. If Regan were really gone forever, one of the Bob-Whites' chief pleasures was gone, too: Mr. Wheeler frequently said that he wouldn't keep the horses if he didn't have someone as knowledgeable and dependable as Regan to take care of them.

More than that, Regan was a good and loyal friend to all the Bob-Whites, always willing to listen to their problems and help them out in any way he could. Trixie, in particular, had good reason to be grateful to Regan. Her six-year-old brother, Bobby, was a favorite of the young groom's, and Regan liked to take over the baby-sitting chores that were among Trixie's usual tasks in the Belden household, leaving Trixie free for the activities the Bob-Whites enjoyed together.

Remembering the sight of Bobby riding "horseback" on Regan's broad shoulders, Trixie felt tears welling in her eyes as she reached the clubhouse.

Pausing before she opened the door, Trixie took a deep breath and swallowed hard. Honey had sounded so upset over the telephone. It wouldn't do for Trixie to walk into the clubhouse in tears, upsetting her even more.

Opening the clubhouse door, Trixie almost lost her composure once again when she saw Honey sitting at the big table in the center of the room, her face in her hands, while Dan Mangan stood behind her, his hand resting on her shoulder.

Dan! Trixie thought, suddenly realizing how selfish she had been not to think about how Regan's nephew must be feeling. *Especially since Regan is the only relative Dan has in the world, since his mother, Regan's sister, died several years ago.* Dan had fallen in with a bad crowd in New York City after his mother's death, but Regan had brought him to live in Sleepyside, and now Dan, too, was a Bob-White.

As Trixie closed the door behind her, both Honey and Dan started and turned to look at her. Trixie could see that Honey's huge hazel eyes were puffy and red-rimmed. Dan's face was white and strained under his unruly dark hair.

Trixie fought to keep her face from showing her own fear. "Where's Regan?" she asked. "What's this all about?"

"We don't know," Honey said. "The last time I saw Regan was this morning in the stable when I went for a ride. He scolded me for not exercising the horses yesterday, but that's not unusual." Honey smiled wryly, and Trixie smiled back. Regan was a good friend to the Bob-Whites, but his horses came first. That dedication, combined with the fiery temper that matched his red hair, often made him impatient with the Bob-Whites when they found "more important" things to do than giving the horses their morning workout.

"Then," Honey continued, "Dan came over this afternoon with the note."

"What note?" Trixie demanded.

"Here," Dan said, handing Trixie a folded piece

of narrow-lined notebook paper.

Unfolding the paper, Trixie immediately recognized Regan's large, bold handwriting. She read the note aloud:

> "Dear Dan,
>   "When you find this, I'll already be gone. I have some things to take care of that may keep me away from the Manor House for quite some time. I wish I could tell you more, but, for the time being, I have to keep 'seecruds,' as Bobby Belden would say.
>   "Please believe that I'll be back as soon as I can. Until then, work hard for Mr. Maypenny, and keep making me proud of you.
>
> >   "Your uncle,
> >   "Regan"

Trixie's voice cracked as she finished reading the note. It was so like Regan, she thought, to want Dan to know how proud he was that his nephew had broken off with the street gang and was now working for Mr. Maypenny, the Wheelers' gamekeeper, in return for room and board. Yet it was so like him, too, to sign the letter "Your uncle," instead of "love."

"When Dan showed me the note, I asked Miss Trask to let us into Regan's apartment above the garage," Honey said. "Everything looked just as it always has—neat as a pin. Only Regan's shaving things and some of his clothes were missing. There was a note on his nightstand addressed to Daddy. My parents had left for Saratoga this afternoon, so Miss Trask opened the letter."

Trixie nodded. Miss Trask was officially Honey's governess, but since Honey had grown more and more independent, Miss Trask had gradually taken on the responsibilities involved in running the Manor House when the Wheelers were away— which was quite often. "What did the note to your father say?" Trixie asked.

Honey shrugged. "It was practically the same as Dan's. He didn't say anything more about where he was going, or why. He did ask Daddy to try to keep his job for him until he got back, but he said he'd understand if Daddy hired someone else."

Trixie suddenly realized that she'd been holding her breath in suspense while she listened to Honey. Now she let it out in a long, helpless sigh. "I wish Jim were here," she said. "And Brian." Brian was the oldest of the four Beldens, and his calm, logical mind often saw solutions to problems that Trixie, in her impatience, overlooked.

"In fact," Trixie added with a lopsided grin, "right now I'd even be happy to see Mart." Mart Belden was her "almost-twin." He was eleven months older than Trixie, but they looked enough alike to be real twins. Trixie delighted in teasing him with the fact that for one month out of the year they were the same age.

Mart, on the other hand, delighted in teasing
Trixie, period. Their constant verbal battles hid the
fact that they were actually devoted to one another.

"But Jim and Brian and Mart *aren't* here,"
Honey pointed out. "They're all counselors at
camp, and they won't be back for a whole week.
Oh, Trixie, what are we going to do?"

"We'll *think*," Trixie said firmly. "Our brothers
aren't the only Bob-Whites who have mastered that
skill, in spite of what they try to tell us. Now, try to
remember if anything unusual happened today,
before Regan disappeared."

Dan Mangan immediately shook his head. "I
hadn't seen Regan since yesterday. He seemed fine
then. He must have left—left the note—while I was
out patrolling the game preserve this afternoon."

Honey shrugged. "I didn't see Regan this afternoon, either. I was busy helping my parents enter-
tain a guest for lunch, a Mr. Worthington, who's
planning to sell my parents another horse.

"Wait a minute!" Honey added, raising her head
so fast that her honey-blond hair bounced on her
shoulders.

"What is it, Honey?" Trixie asked quickly. "Did
you remember something that happened this afternoon?"

"I certainly did," Honey replied. "It has to do
with our guest, Mr. Worthington. I told Regan this
morning that he was coming out here and that he

was a very important horse breeder who owned racing Thoroughbreds. But when the time came to show Mr. Worthington through the stables this afternoon, Regan wasn't around. Tom Delanoy said he'd gone into town to buy some leather to repair a broken piece of tack."

Trixie whistled softly. "You mean Regan knew that someone would be coming around to inspect *his* stable, *his* tack, and the horses *he's* in charge of, and Regan wasn't there to give him the grand tour?"

Honey nodded solemnly. "That's right, Trixie. That isn't like Regan at all."

"I'll say," Dan agreed. "Regan is a very proud man, and the thing he's proudest of is the way he keeps up the horses and everything around them. He doesn't trust strangers not to frighten the horses when he's not around—even if the strangers are supposed to be 'experts.' "

"Now that I think about it," Honey said slowly, "it was right after I told Regan that Mr. Worthington was coming here for lunch that he snapped at me for not exercising the horses yesterday. I didn't think anything about it at the time, because that's not really unusual for Regan. But now—well, I just can't help but wonder if the two things are somehow connected."

The three Bob-Whites sat lost in thought for a long moment. Dan Mangan was the first to break the silence that had settled over the clubhouse. "The two things aren't necessarily connected," he said. "And neither one is necessarily connected with my uncle's disappearance. Maybe Regan really did go to town to buy a piece of leather. As I said, Regan's proud of the way he keeps up the stable. He might have wanted to repair a broken piece of tack before Mr. Worthington came around. In that case, his leaving might have something to do with what happened while he was in town."

"You're right, Dan," Honey said. "Your explanation is just as good as mine. That leaves us right back where we started."

"I don't think so," Trixie said slowly. "I just have a hunch that Honey is right—that Regan's *dis*appearance is connected with the *appearance* of this Mr. Worthington in some way. What else do you know about him, Honey?"

"Very little," Honey admitted helplessly. "He has a lot of money, which he got through speculating on stocks and real estate. He owns Worthington Farms, near Saratoga. His horses race at Saratoga, Belmont, and Churchill Downs." Honey ticked off the points on her fingers as she spoke. "He got in touch with Daddy because he'd heard that Daddy will sometimes buy an injured Thoroughbred, because he's seen too many horses destroyed when their owners made them run to pay for their keep.

"That's really all I know," Honey concluded. "I'd never met Mr. Worthington until this morning, and I don't think my parents had, either."

"Could we ask your parents about him?" Trixie asked.

Honey shook her head. "Not until tomorrow morning when they telephone. I told you, Trixie. They went to Saratoga this afternoon. They drove up with Mr. Worthington."

"That's right," Trixie said. "Well, I can't wait until tomorrow to try to solve this mystery. If this Mr. Worthington is as rich as you say he is, and if his horses have raced at the biggest racetracks in the country, he's probably had magazine articles—or even books—written about him. I say we should go to the Sleepyside library tonight and try to find out more about him."

"Now, hold on, Trixie," Dan said sternly. "Jim, Brian, and Mart are gone, so I'll say the same thing they'd say if they were here. I know how much you love solving mysteries, and I know that you and Honey plan to open the Belden-Wheeler Detective Agency when you finish school. I think you'll be great detectives, too."

Trixie blushed to the roots of her sandy hair, partly because of Dan's praise, which was as rare as his uncle's, but also because she knew what he was going to say next.

"That's right, Trix," Dan said, reading her

thoughts. "I'm going to say that you shouldn't rush into this latest 'mystery.' My uncle has been taking care of himself for a long, long time. There's no reason to think that he can't continue to do so.

"We don't really have any reason to believe he needs any help. After all," Dan said, forcing a grin, "Regan disappeared once before, if you'll remember, and he came back with me! That wasn't so bad, was it?"

"Oh, no, Dan!" Trixie said hastily. "I'm awfully glad he did. And I admit that you're right. I may be jumping to conclusions. Still. . . ."

Dan sighed. "All right, Trixie. I'm pretty worried about Regan, too. The library it is."

Trixie jumped to her feet. "Everybody meet at my house after supper. Bring your bikes. We'll ride to the library and see what we can find out." Looking at her friends' worried faces, she thought, *I hope we find something—something that will lead us to Regan.*

A Troubled Dinner · 2

LEAVING THE CLUBHOUSE, Trixie saw that the sun was much lower in the west than it had been when she went inside. *Gleeps! I bet Moms has dinner almost ready, and I promised her I'd help!* Once again, Trixie set off along the path between the clubhouse and Crabapple Farm at a trot.

When Trixie burst through the kitchen door, the aroma of fried chicken and green beans cooked with onions and bacon told her that dinner was, in fact, almost ready to be served.

"I'm sorry, Moms," she said. She hugged her mother, who stood at the stove stirring the simmering gravy. "I had no idea it was so late."

"It's not *too* late, Trixie," her mother replied calmly. "I managed to leave setting the table and making some instant iced tea for you to take care of." Seeing her daughter's worried look, she asked, "What's the matter, Trixie?"

"Yeah, Trixie, what's the matter?" piped Bobby Belden. Bobby made it a point to always be near the center of activity in the Belden household, and tonight he was making crayon squiggles in a coloring book while his mother bustled around the kitchen.

Trixie almost blurted out the whole story, but she bit her lower lip to keep the words from tumbling out. It wouldn't do to have Bobby find out that his friend Regan had disappeared—not now, when Trixie was still so upset that she might make the situation sound worse than it was. Instead, she paused a moment to catch her mother's eye. "It's nothing," she said, tilting her head almost imperceptibly toward her younger brother.

An equally subtle nod from her mother told Trixie that the subject would be dropped for now and brought up later, when Bobby was out of earshot.

She had forgotten about the sixth sense that Bobby seemed to have for things he wasn't supposed to know about. "Were you at the Manor House, Trixie?" he demanded. "Did you see Regan? Did he tell you to say hello to me, Trixie? He *always* tells you to say hello to me. Regan's my very best friend in the whole world!"

Trixie gathered her brother in her arms and hugged him. She felt as if putting her arms around him might somehow protect him from the truth—that his friend had disappeared, and no one knew where he had gone or why. "I wasn't at the Manor House," she said, "so I didn't see Regan. But if I had, I'm sure he would have told me to say hello. He *is* a good friend, Bobby—to all of us."

Bobby wriggled out of Trixie's arms and went happily back to his coloring book. Trixie hurried to the cupboard, took down the big glass pitcher, and began to make the iced tea. Out of the corner of her eye, she could see her mother watching her closely, and she knew that Mrs. Belden had guessed that Trixie's unhappiness was somehow tied to the Wheelers' groom. *I wish I could tell her all about it now*, Trixie thought.

With a sigh, Trixie busied herself with the last-minute preparations for dinner, trying to keep herself from thinking about Regan. That seemed to be impossible. Her thoughts kept returning to the handsome, red-haired man who had left the Manor House so abruptly.

Trixie had to admit that, as well as she knew Regan, she knew very little *about* him. He'd lived above the garage ever since he moved to the Manor House with the Wheelers. He went out riding every day, exercising the horses. He probably knew the trails that wound through Mr. Wheeler's game preserve better than anyone except Mr. Maypenny, who for years and years had owned a little pie-shaped piece of land in the middle of what was now the preserve.

But Regan almost never went into Sleepyside because he hated both driving and riding in automobiles. And as far as Trixie knew, he had only once gone farther away than that since he'd worked at the Manor House. *That was when he brought Dan back from New York City*, she thought. *Maybe his leaving this time is related*. She shook her head. If Regan had gone off on family business, surely he would have told Dan about it.

Trixie searched her mind for some other clue to Regan's disappearance. He loved sports, but he certainly wouldn't have left such a mysterious note if he were just going to see a baseball game.

It would take something really important to get Regan to leave those horses, Trixie thought. *But what?*

In her mind, she suddenly heard Regan's voice. There was something he'd said to her after he'd first seen Jim Frayne. Jim had been hiding from everyone except Honey and Trixie, afraid that the police would return him to his stepfather. Regan had immediately spotted Jim as a runaway, and Trixie and Honey had thought he'd demand that they tell their parents about Jim.

He hadn't, though. He hadn't said why, not in so

many words, but— *What was it he* did *say?* Trixie thought. She closed her eyes, trying to remember his exact words. Finally they came to her.

"It wasn't so very long ago that I was hiding out in barns myself, wondering where in the world the next meal was coming from." That's what he'd said. Why had Regan been hiding? It was only now that she realized she'd never asked.

Bobby's shrill voice shouting, "Daddy's home!" interrupted Trixie's thoughts, and she hurried to help her mother put the rest of the food on the table. "I'll have to ask Dan if he knows," she muttered to herself.

Bobby Belden was very much present during dinner, so Trixie had to force herself to put Regan out of her mind and talk about other things with her family.

Even so, the talk at the dinner table these days was a far cry from the boisterous, teasing chatter that took place when Mart and Brian were at home. When her brothers had left for camp two weeks earlier, Trixie had breathed an exaggerated sigh of relief. "No more teasing from Mart and no more 'Now, Trix, be careful' from Brian. Not for three whole weeks!" she'd rejoiced.

Her joy had soon turned to loneliness and boredom. Trixie didn't realize, when her brothers were at home, how dependent she was on their banter for amusement. Also, all the Bob-Whites relied on them to plan activities.

With Mart, Brian, and Jim at camp, and Dan working for Mr. Maypenny, and Di Lynch visiting her uncle in Arizona, Honey and Trixie had been left on their own. *Much as I love Honey*, Trixie thought, *it would be nice to have somebody else to visit. I'd even help Di baby-sit for her brothers and sisters.*

Di Lynch was the seventh Bob-White. She and her family—which included two young sets of twins, besides Di—had always lived in Sleepyside, but she and Trixie had not become friends until after Di's father had made a fortune practically overnight and moved his family into the mansion on the other side of the Manor House.

It's really partly my fault that Di's gone, Trixie thought. *If I hadn't discovered that her Uncle Monty was a phony uncle—I mean, that her phony Uncle Monty was a phony—and that her real Uncle Monty was her real uncle, then she wouldn't have had anyone to visit in Arizona this summer.*

Mrs. Belden's voice broke through Trixie's confused thoughts. "Time to clear the table, dear."

Trixie started, then stood up. Picking up a half-full bowl of mashed potatoes, she started for the kitchen. "There seems to be a perponderance of leftovers, as Mart would say."

"That's probably what Mart *would* say," her mother agreed. "But the word is *pre*ponderance.

Still, I know what you mean. Mart loves food even more than he loves to use big words. When he and Brian are away, I can't seem to scale down my recipes enough to avoid leftovers. However, these mashed potatoes can be turned into potato patties for lunch tomorrow."

"Yummy-yum!" Trixie exclaimed. "You know how I love potato patties. Now I wish I hadn't eaten that second helping of potatoes and gravy tonight, so there'd be more left over for tomorrow!"

Mrs. Belden smiled indulgently. "There'll be plenty." Her face turned somber. "Now, Trixie, while your father is reading the evening funny papers to your brother, why don't you tell me what's happened to Regan?"

Trixie sank into a chair and propped her elbows on the kitchen table. "We don't know what's happened to him, Moms. That's just the problem." Trixie repeated everything that she'd learned that afternoon at the clubhouse. "He's just gone," she concluded sadly.

"I'm sure he'll come back as soon as he can," Mrs. Belden said consolingly. "Regan has always seemed to be very happy here in Sleepyside. Did Honey think that Mr. Wheeler would hold Regan's job for him?"

Trixie nodded. "That's the only good news in the whole thing. Miss Trask told Honey that Regan has loads of vacation and sick time coming. Why, the

only time he's ever taken off was when he went to
get Dan. Miss Trask says there'll be no question of
trying to find a permanent replacement for Regan
until that time is used up. Even then, she says, she'll
give him a leave of absence if he's contacted her to
let her know why he's away."

"Well, then," Mrs. Belden said calmly, "I don't
think we have anything to be alarmed about yet.
We'll just tell Bobby, if he asks, that Regan has
gone on a little vacation, and that he'll probably be
back soon. The last part won't even be a white lie,
because I really believe that he will."

Trixie nodded half-heartedly, but as she picked
up a dish towel and began to dry the dishes her
mother was washing, she realized that she, herself,
didn't really believe that Regan would be back.

*Why, oh, why do Mart and Brian and Jim have
to be away?* Honey and Trixie had found Jim when
he ran away to upstate New York, and at the same
time the two girls had solved the mystery of Mr.
Lynch's stolen trailer, the *Robin*. But ever since
then, the boys had been just as much a part of the
mysteries they'd been involved in as Honey and
Trixie had. *Will Honey and Dan and I be able to
find Regan without their help? I guess all we can do
is try.*

"The library it is," she murmured aloud.

A Shadow from the Past · 3

TRIXIE HAD FINISHED drying the dishes and cleaning up the kitchen, and she was waiting impatiently outside, pacing up and down the front walk, when Honey and Dan rode up the driveway.

"I thought you'd never get here!" she exclaimed.

"Now, Trixie," Honey chided her, "it's not very late at all. In fact, Miss Trask had the cook serve our dinner early, so that I could get away."

"Did you tell her where we were going, and why?" Trixie asked.

Honey nodded. "She just sort of raised one eyebrow when I told her. Then she said, 'I know how fond all of you are of Regan. But please, *please*,

33

Honey, don't become involved in another one of
your mysteries!' "

Trixie giggled at Honey's perfect impersonation
of Miss Trask's low, well-modulated voice. "I just
told Moms that we were going to the library. I
didn't tell her why, but I'd already told her about
Regan's disappearance. That's probably why she
gave me that same 'here-we-go-again' look that
Miss Trask gave you."

"I can't understand why they'd think that we
were about to get involved in solving a mystery,"
Dan Mangan said sarcastically. "I mean, it isn't as
though it's ever happened before."

Trixie and Honey both laughed self-consciously.
Ever since the two teen-age girls had met and had
been involved with trying to help Jim Frayne find
the fortune his uncle had left him, it seemed that
they were constantly stumbling across mysteries.
Their parents warned them against trying to solve
them—and they often warned each other, too.
Nevertheless, the Bob-Whites already had to their
credit a long string of cases marked "closed."

"It isn't really a laughing matter," Dan said
sternly, although there was still a mischievous
twinkle in his eyes. "You girls have got yourselves
into a lot of trouble trying to solve these mysteries.
If I were your parents, I'd be worried, too."

Trixie and Honey both turned serious as they
remembered some of the narrow escapes they'd

had in the course of their adventures.

"I know you're right, Dan," Trixie confessed. "And I promise, I won't ever let it happen again. When—*if* I ever again uncover another mystery, I promise I'll run straight to the nearest police officer—

"Wait a minute, Dan!" Trixie interrupted herself, almost causing Dan to fall off his bike in his confusion. "Speaking of running reminded me of something I was going to ask you about—something Regan once said to Honey and me. It was about his having been a runaway himself, when he was just about Jim's age. Do you know why he was running or what he was running from?"

Dan shook his head. "We've never talked much about the past—his or mine. Those are unpleasant memories for both of us. But Regan was an orphan, just as I was. If you knew much about the kinds of places they let orphans live in, you wouldn't have to ask why he ran away. Those places can be pretty depressing."

Sensitive Honey shuddered. "I remember reading *Oliver Twist* a few years ago. That was back before we moved to Sleepyside, when I was always away from my parents, at boarding school and summer camps, and before I had Jim for a brother. I had nightmares for weeks.

"Finally Miss Trask, who was my math teacher back then, noticed how pale and tired I looked and asked me what was wrong. I burst into tears and told her that I was afraid something might happen to my parents while they were on one of their trips. Then I'd be an orphan, just like poor Oliver, I told her, and I'd have to go to one of those dreadful places." Honey looked as though she might burst into tears again, remembering that long-ago incident.

"Orphanages today aren't like the ones that Dickens wrote about, Honey," Dan told her. "You have plenty to eat and a warm bed to sleep in. What's missing, I guess, is a feeling that you belong . . . that somebody loves you.

"So, Trixie," Dan concluded, "maybe Regan wasn't running *away* from anything at all. Maybe he was running *toward* something—a home, like the one he found with the Wheelers."

"Then it makes even less sense that he would have left it so mysteriously, unless something really awful happened," Trixie pointed out. Bending low over the handlebars of her bike, she began to pedal as hard and as fast as she could. "Come on!" she called back over her shoulder to Honey and Dan. "Let's get to the library and try to find out what this is all about."

The effort that it took to keep up their fast pace made it impossible for the three Bob-Whites to talk. Trixie, left once again to her thoughts, found memories of another bike ride into Sleepyside returning to her mind. On that ride, all of the Bob-Whites had been together, leading the other riders back into Sleepyside at the conclusion of the bikeathon. The night before, Trixie had been captured by a gang of counterfeiters. Nick Roberts, the young artist whose need for art supplies had inspired the bikeathon, had helped her to escape.

I wonder if this mystery will end as happily as that one did, Trixie mused.

At the library, Trixie headed straight for the card catalog. Looking through the cards in the section marked "Horse Racing," she copied down a few of the Dewey decimal numbers on a piece of scratch paper and headed for the shelves where those books would be found.

"It isn't a very scientific way of doing research," Trixie admitted, "but leafing through the books that are out on the shelves takes less patience than reading all the catalog descriptions."

"Just make sure you put the books back exactly where they were, Trixie," Honey warned. "If you're the least bit unsure, put them on one of the carts marked 'To be shelved.' Otherwise, you'll make it harder for the next person to find the books he wants."

Dan Mangan nodded in agreement. "In some big-city libraries, the stacks are all closed to the public, because so many books have been stolen or misplaced. If you want a certain book, you have to ask a librarian to send for it. You can't browse at all."

"I'll be careful," Trixie promised, pulling a book from a shelf. Turning to the index, she quickly scanned the columns for a mention of Worthington or Worthington Farms. "Nothing here," she said, reshelving the book.

Dan, Honey, and Trixie pulled book after book off the shelves. They tried to concentrate only on the task at hand, but the three horse-loving teen-agers were continually distracted by interesting bits of information, which they shared with one another.

"Did you know that Thoroughbreds have existed as a breed for over two hundred and forty years?" Honey asked.

"I didn't know that," Trixie admitted. "I *did* know that Thoroughbreds are a breed of horses, though, which is more than some people do. Why, just the other day, I read an article in which some-one mentioned a 'Thoroughbred Arabian.' What the writer meant was 'purebred Arabian.' "

"Listen to this!" Dan exclaimed. "When a horse is racing, his stride is twenty-six feet long!"

Trixie whistled softly, while Honey, conscious of the Sleepyside librarian's love of silence, rounded her lips in a silent "Oh!"

"And," Dan continued, "with every stride, the horse's entire weight of up to twelve hundred pounds is put on one ankle that's only five inches in diameter. That's narrower than some human beings' ankles!"

"It's amazing that the legs don't just snap," Honey said.

"Sometimes they do," Trixie responded sadly, looking up from a passage she was reading. "I was just reading about Ruffian, the filly who had to be destroyed after she broke her leg during a match race."

"Here's a picture of Native Dancer, who won twenty-one of his twenty-two major races, and only lost the Kentucky Derby when another horse bumped against him. Isn't he beautiful?" Honey held the picture up for the others to see.

"He is beautiful," Trixie said, "but he's not the clue to Regan's disappearance. I'm beginning to doubt that we'll find what we're looking for."

"Well, let's keep looking, anyway," Honey said. "There are lots of books left. I had no idea that there were so many books on horses at the Sleepyside library!"

"There are a lot of people in the area who own and raise horses, Honey—as you should know, since your own father is one of them," Dan pointed out.

"And there are probably just as many people who would love to be *able* to own and raise horses but can't afford to—as I should know, since I used

to be one of them. Of course," Trixie added grand-
ly, "that was before your dear father kindly bought
the Manor House and provided me with more fine
horses to keep exercised than I can possibly find
time for."

Honey began to giggle uncontrollably at Trixie's
impression of a haughty society matron, in-
congruous as it was coming from a freckle-faced
teen-ager in a T-shirt and faded blue jeans.

Trixie began to giggle, too, and the librarian
began to give the girls disapproving looks as Dan
tried his best to shush them without making any
more noise—and without breaking out into laughter himself.

At last Trixie and Honey brought their giggling
under control. But Trixie was still struggling to
keep another peal of laughter from breaking
through as she reached to the shelf and took down a
book called *Off the Track*.

*Sounds more like a book about railroad ac-
cidents*, she thought, until she saw the subtitle:
*Behind the Scenes in the World of Professional
Horse Racing*.

Turning to the index, Trixie ran her finger down
the page. She felt her stomach tighten as the name
"Worthington" jumped off the page at her.

"This is it," she told the others in an excited
whisper. "There are two pages in this book about
Mr. Worthington!"

She led the way to a table, sat down, and opened the book to the page listed in the index.

Trixie felt goose bumps rise on her arms when she saw the chapter heading at the top of the page. "Sport of Kings—and Rogues," it said. Afraid to read what was said about Mr. Worthington, she turned to the first page of the chapter and read through it rapidly.

"What's it about, Trix?" Dan asked impatiently.

"It—it's about racetrack scandals," Trixie said. "This author says that racing has always been the most affected by scandals of any major sport, mainly because betting is the backbone of racing. From what this writer says, there must be almost as many ways to cheat at horse racing as there are horses."

"What does the writer have to say about Mr. Worthington?" Honey asked. "I hope he's not a criminal or something."

To Dan and Honey's surprise, the usually daring Trixie slammed the book shut. Her freckles stood out on her face, which was drained of color. "I can't look," she said. "I—I don't know why. It's just a feeling. But I'm afraid to read the part about Mr. Worthington."

Dan snatched the book away from Trixie and turned again to the pages on Mr. Worthington. "You're being silly, Trixie," he said. "We've spent all this time at the library trying to find just this information. This is no time to chicken out.''

Dan began to read the passage aloud. Trixie kept her eyes lowered, staring at the maze of initials carved in the library table by generations of Sleepyside youngsters.

'' 'One scandal of recent years stands out in the mind of this writer as a perfect example of the kind of thing that gives professional horse racing a bad name,' '' Dan read.

'' 'The incident involved Gadfly, an exceptionally talented two-year-old owned by J. T. Worthington of Saratoga, New York.

'' 'The colt was undefeated in his first seven races, and many experts picked him to win racing's Triple Crown as a three-year-old.' ''

''The Triple Crown,'' Trixie breathed. ''That's the Kentucky Derby, the Belmont Stakes, and the Preakness. Only a few horses have ever won the Triple Crown!''

''What happened, Dan?'' Honey asked.

'' 'Gadfly won his eighth race by more than five lengths—a decisive margin,' '' Dan read. '' 'Then, after the race, when the tests that are now required by law at most major racetracks were taken, traces of a drug known to deaden pain in injured horses were found in Gadfly's blood and urine.' ''

''Oh, no!'' Honey gasped.

''That would force the track officials to disqualify Gadfly, wouldn't it?'' Trixie asked.

Dan nodded. "The book also says the horse's owner and the trainer, and Gadfly himself, were barred from all the major tracks in the country for six months for violating the racing code. But that's not all. Listen. 'As so often happens with high-strung, sensitive horses that are bred to race, the banishment seemed to break Gadfly's spirit. Although he was entered in four other races in the following season, Gadfly never again won a race.'"

"Can that really happen?" Trixie asked.

"Yes, it can," Honey said. "Thoroughbreds really are as sensitive as this writer says they are. They'll often race when they're hurt, even when their legs are broken, to keep from losing."

"Is that all the book says about Gadfly, Dan?" Trixie asked.

Dan, who had been reading rapidly down the page, shook his head. "I wish it were. But the worst is yet to come. 'Although Gadfly was retired to Worthington Farms and may yet sire future generations of winning horses, what makes this particular scandal so awful in this writer's memory is that no one was ever brought to justice for his part in what took place.

" 'Perhaps because the incident did not result in any loss of life—human or animal—neither the horse's owner nor the Thoroughbred Racing Protective Association took the necessary measures

to insure that the case would be thoroughly in-
vestigated.' "

Dan took a deep breath before he continued.
" 'This despite the fact that the chief suspect, a
young groom, should have been easy to spot in any
crowd because of his bright red hair!' "

Trixie's Plan • 4

FOR THE SECOND TIME in a few minutes, the book was slammed shut—this time by Dan Mangan. As the sound echoed in the quiet of the library, Dan sat rigidly still, holding the book so tightly that his knuckles turned white. His head lowered, he stared at the front cover as though something fascinating were written on it. Only the tensed muscles of his jaw and the movement of his Adam's apple as he swallowed showed that he was not reading but trying to bring his emotions under control.

When the slamming sound died away, a breathless silence descended over the part of the library where the Bob-Whites sat. The girls, too, sat with their heads lowered, lost in their own thoughts, not wanting to catch each others' eyes and see the fear that would be visible in them.

Unconsciously, Trixie traced with her thumbnail an initial that had been carved in the library table by some restless student. Her thoughts were occupied by a confused jumble of images: a beautiful three-year-old colt galloping across a finish line, the pack of horses far behind him; the same colt, his spirit broken, struggling in the pack in later races while another horse surged ahead.

Mixed with those images were memories of Regan: Regan with Bobby on his shoulders, playing horse; Regan lost in concentration while he curried Lady until her coat was sleek and shining or while he dug a stone out of the tender pad of Starlight's foot; Regan looking stern as he warned the girls about cooling down their horses after a ride.

Suddenly a nightmare image leaped into Trixie's mind: Regan, his face contorted into a villain's mask, a hypodermic syringe in his hand, walking in slow motion toward the stall where Gadfly waited before his race.

The vision was so awful that Trixie gasped. She looked up quickly from the table and glanced around the library, wanting to reassure herself that she was safe in Sleepyside, not living in some nightmare world.

Honey and Dan both looked up when Trixie

gasped, and they both saw the look of stark terror on her face. Dan reached across the table and put his hand on her arm, giving it a gentle, reassuring squeeze.

Trixie looked at Dan and said, in a high, choked voice that belied the hopefulness of her words, "He doesn't give the groom's name, after all. Maybe—" She broke off as Dan shook his head and looked back down at the table. Blushing as she realized how foolish she sounded, she turned to look at Honey.

Honey, too, shook her head. "There can't be much doubt about who the redheaded groom was, Trixie," she admitted. Then, turning to Dan, she added, "But the fact that the writer doesn't mention him by name probably means something else: That the writer wasn't sure enough of the facts to name Regan, that it was just his opinion that Regan doped the horse. But that opinion is wrong— absolutely wrong!" Honey's usually gentle hazel eyes snapped with anger, and her usually quiet voice rose as she spoke.

"That's a good point, Honey," Trixie said eagerly. "There are all kinds of laws about libel and slander. A writer can be sued if he says something that he can't prove to be true about someone. The man who wrote this book is obviously upset about what happened to Gadfly. You can tell that from the way he wrote the chapter. So maybe he just put

in the part about knowing who was the chief suspect to make it seem even worse that Mr. Worthington and the racing association didn't try
hard enough to solve the crime."

Trixie and Honey both looked relieved as they
thought about this new theory, but Dan continued
staring glumly at the table. Trixie leaned forward
to speak to him, then saw the stern face of the
librarian at the desk behind him.

Lowering her voice to a whisper, she said, "Let's
go outside where we can talk about this." In her
haste to leave the library without a confrontation
with the librarian, Trixie rose too quickly and hit
the back of the chair seat with her leg, sending the
chair tumbling backward to the floor with a re-
sounding crash.

Flustered, Trixie whirled around to set it upright,
got tangled in the chair legs, and tumbled to the
floor.

The nervousness that Honey had been feeling
since Dan had finished reading suddenly erupted in
a fit of nervous giggling, and she could only stand
helplessly, clutching her stomach, as she watched
Trixie struggling to untangle herself.

It was Dan who finally grabbed one of Trixie's
flailing arms, pulled her to her feet, and righted the
chair. He, too, was struggling to suppress his
laughter as he said, "I'll put these books back on
the shelves. You two go wait outside for me, before

one of you pulls this ancient building down on top of us."

Trixie, too, had begun to giggle, and she could only nod agreement as she and Honey turned and walked as quickly as possible to the door of the library, carefully avoiding meeting the librarian's astonished and reproachful look.

Once outside, Trixie and Honey sank down on the steps of the library and continued to laugh until the tears rolled down their cheeks.

Finally Trixie's laughter subsided, and a woeful look replaced the mirthful one. "Why am I such a clumsy oaf, Honey? And how can I laugh when everything is so—so absolutely awful?"

Honey hugged her friend sympathetically. "Don't feel bad, Trixie. You aren't clumsy at all, except when you get impatient and try to move too fast, the way you did just now. It doesn't happen very often—at least, not anymore. But we've all teased you a lot for being clumsy when it *does* happen, so we've made you self-conscious about it. That's our fault, and I'm going to talk to the boys about it.

"And as for laughing at a time like this, that's normal, too. People can't keep emotions bottled up inside for very long. They have to come out some way, in laughing or crying or something. It can be embarrassing, but it's normal, and usually people understand."

Trixie shook her head. "Maybe you understand, Honey, because you're so *understanding*. But I don't understand myself when I act the way I did in there just now. And Dan must think I'm awful, making a fool of myself and then giggling as though everything were wonderful, when his only relative in the whole world might possibly be in serious trouble."

"I don't think you're awful at all, Trixie," Dan said, sitting down on the step beside her. "I know that you're worried about Regan. We all are."

"*I'm* not as worried now as I was before we went to the library," Honey said. "In fact, I think our mystery is pretty much solved."

Trixie and Dan both gave Honey bewildered looks.

"Don't you see?" she asked them. "When Daddy told Regan that Mr. Worthington was coming to visit the Manor House, Regan realized that he might be accused of giving the drugs to Gadfly, which of course he didn't do. So he just went away until Mr. Worthington left."

Trixie shook her head. "I'm afraid it's not that simple, Honey. Remember, Regan's note said he had 'things to take care of.' Leaving the Manor House just to avoid running into Mr. Worthington wouldn't take care of anything. I think he's gone off to try to solve the mystery once and for all, to clear himself."

"Or to turn himself in," Dan muttered.

Trixie turned on Dan angrily. "That's a terrible thing to say, Dan Mangan! I don't even know how you can say it, knowing Regan as well as you do. Even if you didn't know him so well, you might try remembering that he showed a lot more faith in you when he first brought you to Sleepyside, and he hardly knew you at all!"

"I'm sorry," Dan said immediately. "You're right, of course, Trixie. I don't know why I said that. I guess it's just that so many of the people I knew before I came here turned out to be bad characters. I know, now, that people can be good, but sometimes it's hard for me to keep that kind of faith."

"We understand, Dan," Honey said quickly. "People's past experiences always affect the way they see things. Trixie and I, because of our past, tend to be too trusting, and that's got us into some dangerous situations sometimes. But the main thing right now is to keep believing that Regan is innocent."

Once again, Trixie shook her head. "That isn't the main thing, Honey. Just believing in Regan's innocence won't bring him back to Sleepyside, and that's what we have to do."

"But how?" Honey asked.

"Well," Trixie said slowly, "we can either find Regan and convince him that he has to come back, or we can solve the mystery for him so that he'll come back on his own. Or, better still, we can do both!"

"How can we, Trixie?" Honey asked hopelessly. "The mystery that you're talking about is almost seven years old. What we just read didn't give us any clues on how to solve it, and anything that Regan knew, he kept to himself. I wouldn't know where to begin."

Trixie shrugged. "Then we begin by finding Regan," she said.

"Don't be silly, Trixie," Dan said, sounding half-angry at Trixie's confident tone. "You have no idea where he went or where to begin looking."

"We found Jim when he disappeared," Trixie said stubbornly.

"That was different, Trixie," Honey pointed out. "We had a hard enough time finding Jim, and we almost got killed in the process, but at least we'd some idea where to start looking, because Jim had mentioned going to look for work at a boys' camp in upstate New York."

"Exactly," Trixie agreed. "And Regan said in his note that he had 'things to take care of,' and we now know—or at least we're fairly sure—that those things have to do with Mr. Worthington and Gad-fly and a race that took place seven years ago at Saratoga. So—"

"That's it!" Honey interrupted, snapping her

fingers as she finally understood the point that Trixie had been leading up to. "Regan went to Saratoga!"

"Well, that makes everything easy as pie," Dan said sarcastically. "You can just take the contents of the Bob-Whites' treasury, which amount to about three dollars, as I recall, and use it to go to Saratoga to look for Regan."

"We don't have to!" Honey said joyfully, ignoring Dan's sarcasm. "Remember, Dan? My parents are in Saratoga right now. When they call tomorrow, I'll ask if we can come up and join them there!"

"Oh, Honey, that's wonderful!" Trixie exclaimed, throwing her arms around her friend. Then she added, seriously, "But you'd better not tell them our reasons for wanting to come to Saratoga. You know how our parents feel about our trying to solve mysteries on our own. Just tell them we're getting bored silly in Sleepyside, and we'd like to have a vacation to talk about when the boys get home ready to lord it over us with stories about their adventures at camp."

Honey giggled. "That certainly is the, truth, Trixie—even if it's not the *whole* truth. Oh, I can hardly wait to find Regan!"

"Then let's get home before dark, or our parents will ground us and we won't even be able to go to the mailbox, let alone to Saratoga!" Trixie said. She jumped up from the step and ran toward the bike rack. Honey followed eagerly, but Dan, still un-convinced that Trixie's plan was a workable one, walked slowly and thoughtfully behind.

"The Trip Is On!" • 5

ALTHOUGH TRIXIE went to bed almost as soon as she got home, the day's excitement had left her wide-awake. She tossed and turned for hours, wishing she'd checked a book out of the library to read until she felt sleepy. That thought reminded her again of the chair-tipping incident, and she felt her cheeks grow hot as she pictured herself sprawled across the floor. "I'm glad Mart wasn't there to see me make a fool of myself," she murmured into the darkness. "He'd never let me forget it."

Then, not wanting to speak the words out loud, even in the privacy of her room, she thought, *I'm glad Jim wasn't there, either.* All of the Bob-Whites

knew about the special friendship that existed between Jim and Trixie, and it, too, was a cause for
teasing from Mart Belden. Trixie firmly denied to
the other Bob-Whites, and usually to herself, as
well, that Jim was a "boyfriend." Still, she had to
admit that, at times, his opinion of her was more
important than that of anyone outside her family.

"Except Honey's," she murmured. "But that's
different. Honey and I are so close, and she's such a
loyal person, anyway, that I don't worry about losing her friendship—even when I *ought* to worry,"
she added wryly, remembering the time when she
and Honey had stopped speaking because of Trixie's suspicions of Honey's cousin Ben Ryker.

Groaning, Trixie rolled over on her side and pulled
the pillow over her head, as if to silence her own
thoughts. *I'll never get to sleep if I just let myself
keep jumping from one memory to another*, she
thought.

She rolled onto her back and, putting the pillow
under her head, began a relaxing exercise she'd
read about. Starting with her toes and working upward, she tensed and then relaxed her muscles, con-
centrating on the muscles and keeping her mind a
blank. Finally, she drifted off to sleep.

Trixie woke with a start, sat bolt upright in her
bed, and gasped for breath. She looked around the
room, only gradually coming out of the nightmare

she'd just been dreaming and returning to the real
world, where everything was familiar, even the
bright patch of morning sunlight on the foot of her
bed.

She closed her eyes and sank back on her pillow,
remembering the dream. She'd been walking
through a crowd of people when she'd spotted
Regan's red head in the distance. She'd called his
name, but he hadn't seemed to hear her. Struggling
through the crowd, she'd come to a road and spotted Regan walking away from her. She'd begun to
run, harder and faster than she ever had in her life,
but she couldn't seem to catch up to him.

Finally, in a burst of speed, she had caught up to
him. She had thrown her arms around him and
said, "Oh, Regan, I'm so glad I found you!" But
just then, a man had appeared from nowhere. He'd
been wearing a dark suit, with a badge on the lapel
that said "Track Official." "You're disqualified!"
he'd shouted, and while Trixie had tried to understand what he meant, Regan had disappeared.

"And I woke up," Trixie murmured. "What a
wonderful way to start the morning." Sighing, she
got out of bed.

By the time Trixie started her morning chores,
she was already waiting impatiently for Honey's
phone call, and her spirits were almost as low as
Dan's had been the night before.

"You're just tired," she told herself as she changed

the sheets on her bed. "Otherwise, you wouldn't be
so worried about a silly old dream." Gathering up
the sheets she'd just taken off the bed, she rolled
them into a ball in her arms, marched to the laun-
dry chute, and threw them down, as if she were trying to throw the memory of the dream away with
them.

But it wasn't that easy to put the nightmare out
of her mind. She vacuumed and dusted with her
mind only partly on her work.

She was standing with the dustrag in her hand,
gazing across the living room at the telephone and
wishing it would ring, when she felt a tug on her
sleeve and looked down into the worried gaze of
her little brother.

"I need a glass of water, Trixie," Bobby said. "I
need it bad, and I asked you twice, but you didn't
hear me. What's wrong, Trixie?"

"I'm sorry, Bobby. I—I was thinking about something else. Let's go get some water."

"What were you thinking about, Trixie?" Bobby
demanded as they walked into the kitchen.

Mrs. Belden looked up from the bread dough she
was kneading and smiled. "I've been wondering
the same thing all morning, Bobby," she said. "I
suspect that while your sister's hands are doing
dusting and vacuuming here in Sleepyside, her
mind is far away, at a certain boys' camp in
upstate New York."

"What does that mean?" Bobby asked, looking from his mother to his older sister in confusion.

Laughing, Trixie gave Bobby a hug as she told him, "Moms means that I miss Brian and Mart and Jim."

"Oh," Bobby said solemnly. "I understand *that*. I miss them, too, Trixie. I miss them something *awful*."

"I'm going to remind you both of what you just said when your brothers get back and the four of you begin teasing each other, as you always do. And, although I haven't been able to hear what your brothers have said this summer, I feel fairly sure that they—and Jim—have also admitted to missing the two of you."

Trixie wrinkled her nose. "I doubt that," she said. "If we could overhear that terrible trio, we'd probably hear them saying that they wish they could spend the rest of their lives at camp, away from chores and away from baby-sitting."

Mrs. Belden laughed. "You seem to forget, Trixie, that chores and baby-sitting are exactly what your brothers are doing at camp—and in much larger measure than any of you do here at home."

Trixie giggled. "You're right, Moms. I always think of that camp as a vacation resort for the boys. I forget that they spend a lot of their time doing dishes, sweeping floors, and trying to keep oodles of energetic little boys out of patches of poison ivy."

Trixie and her mother started as the screen door slammed. Trixie hurried over to it and saw Bobby running down the driveway to the mailbox, where the mail carrier's truck had just pulled up.

Smiling, Trixie shook her head. "I don't know how he does it, Moms," she said. "Bobby can hear the mailman's truck coming before it leaves downtown Sleepyside. And yet he never hears me ask him to get cleaned up before dinner."

"That talent for hearing only what they want to hear is one that all of my children seem to have," Mrs. Belden teased.

"That's true," Trixie admitted. "Why, just a few minutes ago, I was so lost in thought that I didn't hear Bobby ask me for a glass of water." She giggled. "He said he needed it 'bad,' but he forgot all about it when he heard the mailman's truck. There must be something exciting in the mail, because he's running back up the driveway as fast as he can, waving an envelope over his head."

Before Bobby even reached the back step, his mother and sister heard him shout, "It's a letter from Brian and Mart!"

"Yippee!" Trixie yelled, as excited as her six-year-old brother. Then, remembering that Bobby's reading was often questionable, she called, "Are you sure it's from them, Bobby?"

The screen door slammed as Bobby entered the kitchen. " 'Course I'm sure, Trixie," he said, looking hurt. "I know my own name, and my own name is the same as Mart and Brian's own name. At least, the last part is. See?" He pointed at the return address on the envelope, which was already crumpled from being clutched tightly in Bobby's small hand. "This big letter is a *B*. And this little one is an *e*. And the tall skinny letter is an *l*, and—"

"That's very good, Bobby," Trixie interrupted impatiently. "I had no idea you'd learned so many letters. But don't you want to know what Brian and Mart have to say?"

"Oh, yes," Bobby said, remembering that the letter inside the envelope was even more interesting than the letters on the outside. "Will you read it to us, Moms?"

"I will, indeed," Mrs. Belden said, washing her hands at the kitchen sink and drying them before she took the letter from Bobby. She sat down at the kitchen table, and Trixie quickly sat down and pulled Bobby onto her lap.

"The first part of the letter is in Brian's handwriting," Mrs. Belden said. " 'Dear Moms, Dad, Trixie, and Bobby:' " she read. " 'Greetings from your hardworking sons. We've been meaning to write for days, but by the time we're really sure that all of our young monsters are asleep for the night, and not just pretending to be asleep so they can sneak out of the cottage later, we're so tired that we just tumble into our own cots.

" 'In other words, we're working very hard, but we're enjoying every minute of it. We took a two-day canoe trip this week, and Jim impressed everyone with his knowledge of woodlore, while Mart scared everyone—including me and Jim—half-silly with his ghost stories around the campfire.' "

"Mart tells great stories!" Bobby exclaimed.

"He certainly does," Trixie agreed, shivering as she remembered the times, years ago, when she had lain awake in her room after listening to one of Mart's tales, imagining that every shadow was a ghost.

Mrs. Belden, reading ahead, smiled as she said, "The handwriting changes here. See if you can guess who wrote this:

" 'My elder sibling is predictably unostentatious in describing our peregrinations. His ministrations to sunburns and blisters were no less integral to our journey than Jim's forest acumen or my histrionic ability.' "

"I know who wrote it," Bobby said. "Mart did. But I sure don't know what it means!"

Trixie sniffed. "I doubt that Mart knows exactly what all those big words mean, either, Bobby. But I *think* the translation is something like, 'Brian didn't take enough credit for what he did on the trip. He gave first aid to the campers, and that was just as important as Jim's woodlore or Mart's scary stories.' Right, Moms?"

Mrs. Belden nodded and continued reading. " 'Seriously, Moms, I can tell from watching Brian and Jim that we have a good idea in planning to open a school for boys after we all finish college. Brian is going to be a first-rate doctor, and Jim is just wonderful with all the kids up here. Working at this camp is great experience for us, although my teaching of agriculture is limited pretty much to *trying* to make sure that everyone can recognize poison ivy. And I might add that I haven't always succeeded even in that.' "

"Poison ivy—yuch!" Bobby shouted.

"*Yuch* is right," Trixie added. "Go on, Moms."

"There's not much left," Mrs. Belden said. "Just one more paragraph, in Brian's handwriting again. He says, 'Sorry this letter is so short, but we have to hit the hay. The wake-up call comes awfully early around here, and the kids wake up rarin' to go. We're both looking forward to coming home to the soft life at Crabapple Farm next week.' "

"Soft life!" Trixie hooted. "They're not going to have it so soft when I hand over my chores for three weeks, to make up for having done all of theirs since they've been gone."

"That's something you'll have to work out with your brothers," Mrs. Belden said. "Right now, you might be interested in the postscript to this letter."

Taking the letter from her mother, Trixie felt her heart flutter as she recognized Jim's handwriting.

"Dear Trix," she read silently, "I've been writing to Honey and my folks while Brian and Mart wrote this letter, and I'm just as bushed as they are. But I did want to say *hi*. And I wanted to remind you to take care of yourself and not—I repeat, *not*—get involved in any mysteries while we're away. I worry about you, Trixie. We all do."

Trixie felt a wave of guilt. She and Honey had debated, on the way home the night before, whether or not they should telephone the boys and tell them about Regan's disappearance and their decision to go to Saratoga to try to find the missing groom. Honey, who was more willing to admit her feeling of dependence on Jim, had argued for writing to the boys. Trixie had argued against that approach, pointing out that if the boys came home, it would be impossible to convince Honey's parents that their trip to Saratoga was just a vacation. The Wheelers would realize immediately that the girls had asked to go to Saratoga so that they could find Regan, Trixie pointed out. And, more than likely, the result would simply be that the Wheelers would refuse to take any of the Bob-Whites along, ending their chances to find Regan and clear up the mystery.

In the end, it had been Dan who had tipped the scales in favor of not calling Mart, Brian, and Jim. He had reminded the girls of how important working at the camp was to the boys' futures. If they left early, Dan argued, it might be hard for them to get good references from the camp director, and they probably wouldn't get hired again the following year.

Honey, who was always so sensitive to the feelings of others, had quickly agreed that it wouldn't be right to risk ruining the boys' future plans, especially when they didn't really know if they'd succeed in finding Regan.

Now, rereading Jim's note, Trixie found herself wondering if their decision had been a wise one. Then she remembered what Mart had written: "Working at this camp is great experience for us," he had said.

We made the right decision, Trixie thought. *We have no right to spoil that experience for them.*

The phone rang, and Trixie jumped up to answer it. Bobby, who had been sitting quietly on Trixie's lap spelling out the few words he knew in the boys' letter, hollered in protest. "Sorry, Bobby," Trixie said, hugging him quickly before she dashed to the phone.

She paused with her hand on the receiver and whispered, "Please, let it be Honey," then picked up the receiver and said, "Hello?"

"It's all set!" Honey's voice sounded joyously in Trixie's ear. "Daddy called just a few minutes ago. I asked him if we could come up to Saratoga for a few days, and he said it was a wonderful idea. He wondered why he hadn't thought of it himself!"

"That's wonderful, Honey!" Trixie exclaimed.
"Did he invite Dan, too?"

"He did," Honey answered. "But Dan doesn't
feel that he should go. I spoke to him about it this
morning, when he was at the stable working with
the horses. He said he feels that he can help his uncle more by staying here and trying to fill in for
him, so that Regan's job will be waiting for him
when he comes back."

"I suppose that's true, although I wish Dan could
come with us. Gleeps!" Trixie added. "I don't even
know yet that *I* can come along! I'll ask Moms right
now, then I'll call you back to get all the details
about when we're leaving and what I should bring."

Mrs. Belden readily gave Trixie permission to go
with Honey to Saratoga, although she made it clear
that she suspected that Trixie had been waiting for
Honey's call all morning. "I can see that your
thoughts weren't *all* on your brothers at camp," she
said. "But I do think that a vacation will do you
good. It will do me good, too, if it keeps you from
being envious of your brothers' adventures when
they get home."

Trixie threw her arms around her mother's neck.
"Moms, you're the greatest!" she said. "I'll call
Honey right back and tell her the trip is on!"

Trixie and Honey briefly discussed what time
they would leave and what they should pack for the

trip. Honey explained that Tom Delanoy, the Wheelers' chauffeur, would drive them to Saratoga the following morning. Tom's pretty wife, Celia, would go with them. Then Trixie, remembering that her vacation would leave her mother totally without help around the house, hastily said good-bye and threw herself into her chores.

"I just wish there were more I could do in advance," she told her mother. "I keep thinking I should make all the beds seven times in a row, or try to talk a week's worth of weeds to come up in the garden today, so I can pull them out. But that just isn't possible."

"I appreciate all you've done, Trixie," her mother said. "But now I think you should do some things for yourself—like packing your bag."

"Gleeps! That's right!" Trixie exclaimed. "And when I've finished, I'm going straight to bed. I want to get a good night's sleep before I take my vacation!"

But with her suitcase packed, Trixie found herself once again lying sleeplessly in bed, wondering what the next few days would bring. "I've called this trip to Saratoga a 'vacation' so many times that I've begun to believe that's all it is," she said aloud. "But finding Regan and solving the mystery that made him leave Sleepyside is the important thing. I just hope that Honey and I will be able to manage it alone."

The Search Begins · 6

TWO RESTLESS NIGHTS in a row made Trixie oversleep the next morning. When she did wake up, she moved with a slowness that was rare for the usually energetic teen-ager. Consequently, Trixie was still eating breakfast when Honey bounded in through the back door, remembering her manners just in time to catch the screen door before it slammed.

Mrs. Belden shook her head in disbelief. "If you didn't have the same blond hair and hazel eyes, I'd say you couldn't possibly be the same frail, timid little girl who moved in next door not so very long ago, Honey," she said.

"I'm sorry for being so rude, Mrs. Belden," Honey apologized.

"Moms didn't mean you were being rude, Honey," Trixie said. "Just normal. Right, Moms?"

"Exactly," Mrs. Belden agreed. "And I must admit that I'm quite proud of the fact that my own bouncing daughter had a part in the change you've gone through."

Honey giggled. "Trixie had more than a part in the change, Mrs. Belden. She practically caused it single-handedly. When Trixie and I first became friends, I was afraid of my own shadow. But Trixie isn't afraid of anything. And since I was always more afraid of being left alone than I was of following Trixie, I did a lot of things that frightened me at first; then I discovered they weren't so frightening, after all!"

"I just wish," Mrs. Belden said ruefully, "that a little of your caution had rubbed off on Trixie while her fearlessness was rubbing off on you!"

"I give you a lot of worried moments, don't I, Moms?" Trixie asked somberly. "Well, I promise I'll stay out of trouble in Saratoga. So don't worry about me for a minute!"

"Saratoga!" Honey exclaimed. "Do you know, I'd almost forgotten that we were leaving? Tom and Celia are waiting in the car. Tom's too polite to honk the horn, but I'm sure he's getting impatient. Are you ready, Trixie?"

"Sure am!" Trixie responded, carrying her breakfast dishes to the sink and giving them a quick rinse. "My suitcase and purse are right there, by the door." She hugged her mother and younger brother and headed toward the door.

It was Honey who noticed Bobby's forlorn look and trembling chin. She knelt beside his chair and hugged him. "Poor Bobby," she said sympathetically. "You're going to miss your sister, aren't you?"

Bobby nodded sadly. "I'm gonna miss everybody, 'cause everybody's gonna be gone," he said.

"It's only for a week, Bobby," Trixie reassured him. "Then Honey and I will be back, and Mart and Brian and Jim will be home a couple of days after that."

"As soon as we get back, I'll come over and tell you all about what we did and what we saw in Saratoga," Honey promised. "I'll bring you a souvenir, too. Would you like that?"

To Honey's surprise, Bobby shook his head. "I don't want one of those," he said. "But would you bring me a present?" He looked around, confused as Honey, Trixie, and Mrs. Belden all burst out laughing.

"All right, Bobby," Honey agreed. "I'll bring you a present, instead."

Trixie and Honey were still laughing over Bobby's unintentional humor as they got into the car.

Tom put Trixie's bag in the trunk with Honey's, then started down the driveway before he asked, "What's got you girls laughing so hard this early in the morning?"

When Honey told Tom and Celia what Bobby had said, they laughed, too. "It can't be easy for Bobby, being the youngest in the family," Tom observed. "He gets a lot of love and attention when everyone's around, but he also gets left alone a lot when everyone else has places to go and things to do."

Trixie nodded. "I know. I used to feel awfully jealous of Mart and Brian before Honey moved here; they were older and could do more things on their own than I could. I was always asking to come along when they went someplace, but it seemed they always were going someplace I couldn't go because I was too young."

"I'll tell you what," Celia Delanoy said. "I have to go into Sleepyside to do the marketing tomorrow. I'll call your mother and ask if Bobby can ride along when Tom drives me into town. That way he'll feel as though he'd had a small adventure of his own this week, anyway."

"Oh, that'd be wonderful," Trixie said. "I know he'll appreciate it."

"Dan told me he'd try to take Bobby out to see Mr. Maypenny this week, too," Honey said. "But I'm afraid he's going to be a lonely little boy, with all of the Bob-Whites gone, and Regan, too."

"Then there's been no more word from Regan?"
Celia asked.

Honey shook her head. "None so far, I'm afraid."

Trixie cast a worried look at her friend, wondering briefly whether Honey would forget herself and
tell the Delanoys the real reason for their trip to
Saratoga. Seeing Trixie's look, Honey shook her
head, almost imperceptibly, to reassure her that the
secret was safe.

Everyone was silent for a few moments. Tom
watched the road ahead, and Celia and the two
girls stared at the scenery, each lost in her own
thoughts.

Trixie suddenly became aware that Honey was
speaking to her. "I'm sorry, Honey. What did you
say? I was a million miles away."

Honey giggled. "Not that far, I bet. You were
more like a hundred miles away, in Saratoga. I
asked whether you'd had any trouble deciding
what to pack."

Trixie groaned. "Boy, did I ever!" she said. "I
remembered what we'd talked about: comfortable,
casual clothes for the track, one or two nice outfits
in case your parents take us out for dinner, a swimsuit if we want to swim in the hotel pool. Then I
looked through my closet and my dresser drawers
and couldn't find anything that fit that list except
the swimsuit. What I call 'comfortable' isn't just

casual, it's downright ragged. And my nice outfits all have torn seams or missing buttons that I always forget about until those rare occasions when I need to wear them. Finally, I just closed my eyes and grabbed some things and threw them in my suitcase and closed it." Seeing Honey's horrified look, Trixie giggled and added, "I didn't really do that, Honey. But I know that even if I'd gone out and bought all new clothes for the trip, I wouldn't look as nice as you always do."

"Now, now," Tom Delanoy said from the front seat. "You're a very nice-looking young lady, Miss Trixie Belden. And I'm an expert on pretty ladies. After all, I married one."

Celia blushed and smiled, and Trixie laughed. "I have no choice but to accept that compliment gracefully," she said, "since I can't tell you you're wrong, at least not about the woman you married."

"Well, I thank you both," Celia said. "I wouldn't worry about your clothing if I were you, Trixie. For one thing, I don't think you realize how much more grown-up-looking you're becoming. For another thing, you're going to Saratoga to see things, not to be seen parading in pretty clothing."

"Absolutely!" Trixie agreed. "Oh, and I just can't wait. Do you know, even though I've loved horses for as long as I can remember and have ridden almost every day since I've known Honey, I've never seen an honest-to-goodness horse race?"

"You'll love it, Trix," Honey told her. "Our horses are beautiful, of course, and I adore them, but a racing Thoroughbred in top condition is *perfectly perfect*. It isn't just the horses, either, that make Saratoga so much fun. There's so much excitement at the race track. There's a big, lighted board that shows the odds on the horses that are racing, and the numbers are constantly changing as people place bets. And the people! Daddy says a race track has more genuine characters per square foot than anyplace else in the world, and he's absolutely right. Some of them are exactly what you'd imagine, with loud suits and flashy diamond rings. Others you'd expect to see anywhere but at the races—quiet little old ladies, sophisticated older men, and some people who look so ragged you wouldn't expect them to have two dollars to place a bet with. Oh, I can't begin to describe it, Trixie. You'll just have to see it for yourself!"

"I think you describe it very well, Honey," Trixie told her. "I get shivers just listening to you, in fact! I do want to see it myself, though. I want to see all those strange people!" To herself, Trixie added, *I want to see one familiar person, too—Regan!*

When Tom pulled up in front of the hotel where the Wheelers were staying, it was just a few minutes before noon. He carried the bags into the hotel and waited while Trixie and Honey were checked into the room that Mr. Wheeler had reserved for them. The desk clerk handed Honey a note from her parents, telling her that they had had to go to a luncheon with friends.

"Daddy says that we should have lunch in the restaurant here at the hotel. We can sign for it, and they'll just put it on our bill. He says that you and Celia should have lunch with us, Tom, if you'd like to."

"I'm sure that Celia would like to," Tom said. "She's such a good cook that the little dining room in our trailer seems like a gourmet restaurant to me most days, so eating out isn't a big treat for me. But it is for her! I'll go park the car and we'll meet you in the restaurant."

Trixie felt a momentary twinge of impatience. She and Honey had been together all morning without being able to say anything to one another about the real purpose of their trip to Saratoga. Now that they had arrived at the hotel, Trixie wanted only to go to their room and plan their strategy for finding Regan—or at least for finding out what had happened all those years before that had finally caused him to leave the Manor House. *Oh, woe,* she thought. *I don't know how I'll be able to make it through a whole hour without blurting something out to Honey.*

As the thought ran through her mind, Trixie's impatience was replaced with a guilty feeling. *Tom's spending a whole day driving us up here and*

then driving back to Sleepyside, and Celia's spend-
ing her day off to ride along, just so they can be
together. An hour of my time isn't much, when I'm
getting a whole week's vacation. "Come on,
Honey," she said aloud. "Let's go meet Celia and
Tom. I'm starved!"

Trixie and Honey met Tom and Celia in front of
the hotel restaurant, but seeing its dark interior and
lavish furnishings, all four agreed that they'd feel
more comfortable in the brightly lit, less expensive-
looking coffee shop off the lobby. They ordered
sandwiches and iced tea and chatted happily about
Sleepyside, the Manor House, and all of the pleasant experiences that were awaiting the girls at
Saratoga.

When they were ready to leave, Celia's face
clouded as she said, "Maybe it's just because we're
in a town that's famous for its horses, but all morning long I've been thinking about poor Regan. He's
devoted to those horses, and he's always seemed
so loyal to the Wheelers. It must be something very
serious that would make him disappear so—so
mysteriously."

Trixie and Honey both nodded their agreement
without speaking, afraid that they might betray
their plans to find the missing groom.

"Now, Celia," Tom said, patting his wife's arm,
"don't go getting the girls all upset right at the start
of their vacation. I'm sure that Regan is all right

and that he'll be coming back to Sleepyside one day soon." Getting up from the table, he added, "And speaking of getting back to Sleepyside, that's exactly what we should be doing."

Celia rose, too, and smiled at the girls. "I'm sorry if I sounded gloomy," she said. "Don't start worrying about Regan because of what I said."

"We won't," Trixie said truthfully, then added silently, *We started worrying about Regan long before Celia said anything.*

Back in the lobby, Tom told the girls, "Don't go wandering too far by yourselves. I'm sure that the Wheelers will be back soon to give you the grand tour."

"Thank you for the ride, Tom," Trixie said quickly, before Honey could promise to take Tom's advice. "We'll be careful."

"You be careful, too, Tom," Honey said. "I want you and Celia to arrive in Sleepyside safe and sound."

"Tom's the safest driver in the world," Celia said loyally. "Now, you girls have a good time. I won't forget my promise to take Bobby on an outing while you're gone."

With a final wave, Tom and Celia left for the car, and Honey and Trixie walked through the lobby to their room.

Once they were there, each sitting cross-legged on one of the double beds, Trixie realized that all of

the planning she had wanted to do was more dif-
ficult than she had realized.

"I guess I don't even know where to begin,
Honey," she admitted.

"I don't, either, Trix. Even though I've visited
Saratoga with my parents before, I can't really say
that I know the town or anyone who lives here."

The girls sat silent for a moment, each trying
vainly to work out a master plan for finding Regan.

"I give up," Trixie said finally. "All we can do is
plunge in. We have to see as much of the track
behind the scenes as we can and ask as many questions as we can without raising suspicions."

Honey giggled. "Between plunging in and getting behind the scenes, I don't know if we're here to
watch horse races, go swimming, or produce a
play. I think that's what Mart would call a 'mixed
metaphor.' But I also think you're right. We'll just
see all we can and hope a clue turns up soon."

"Right. Let's start right now by going for a
walk," Trixie suggested.

"Oh, Trixie, remember what Tom said?" Honey
reminded her.

"I remember exactly what he said," Trixie
replied. "He said that we shouldn't go wandering
too far. So we'll just walk around a few blocks from
the hotel. Come on!"

"All right," Honey agreed. "But remember, let's
not go far. I'll leave a note at the front desk for my

parents saying that we arrived safely and that we'll be back by four o'clock. That will give us plenty of time to dress for dinner."

Trixie groaned. "If we have to dress for dinner, I'd just as soon get lost forever in Saratoga," she said mournfully.

Laughing, Honey followed her friend out of the room.

A Startling Discovery • 7

As THE TWO GIRLS began to explore Saratoga, Trixie's dread of dressing for dinner vanished, and even their constant anxiety about Regan retreated to the backs of their minds as they savored the charm and history of the town.

The girls walked down the street, pausing to look at shop windows that displayed everything from elegant-looking evening dresses to cheap souvenirs.

"I have to remember to bring something home for Bobby," Trixie said, "but I certainly don't want anything like this. All those ashtrays and pillows and T-shirts are the same for every single city in the country, with only the name changed."

"That's right," Honey said, "and usually, if you look for a label, you discover that your souvenir was actually made in Taiwan or Hong Kong. We'll find something for Bobby that *really* represents Saratoga."

Trixie giggled. "The only thing I can think of that represents Saratoga to me is a racehorse. I don't imagine Moms would be too pleased if we brought a horse home for Bobby."

Honey giggled, too, at the image of the girls walking up the Belden driveway followed by a Thoroughbred stallion. "A racehorse isn't the only souvenir of the track, Trixie. Even a copy of the racing program from the track would be a better, and less expensive, souvenir for Bobby than a horse he couldn't ride. But you're forgetting that the track isn't the only thing that Saratoga is famous for. Saratoga was a very famous town long before there were horse races here."

"The horses are the only thing I know about," Trixie admitted. "What else is Saratoga famous for?"

"Oh, Trixie, don't you remember studying the Battle of Saratoga in American history class? Actually, there were *two* Battles of Saratoga. In the second one, the American soldiers were attacked by the British under General Burgoyne. The Americans forced him to retreat to Saratoga, surrounded him, and finally got him to surrender. That battle is

known as the turning point of the Revolutionary
War. One of the big heroes for the American
side was Benedict Arnold, who was a great general
with the Continental Army before he became a
traitor."

The girls had gradually slowed their steps as
Honey spoke, and now Trixie stood stock-still,
open-mouthed with surprise. "Why, Honey," she
said, "you're no better in American history than I
am. How do you remember so much about the Battle of Saratoga? I mean, I remember studying all
those things, now that you mention them, but I certainly wouldn't have been able to rattle them all off
the way you just did."

Honey laughed and hugged her friend. "You're
forgetting that I had already visited Saratoga with
my parents when we studied 'all those things' in
class. That makes a big difference. To you, the Battle of Saratoga was just words on the page of a text-
book. To me, it was a story about a place I'd visited
and enjoyed. That made it as easy to remember as
the legends of Rip Van Winkle and the early Dutch
settlers, like the ones old Brom told us."

Trixie nodded. "I have no trouble remembering
old Brom's stories. Some of the scarier ones can
keep me awake at night even now, if I happen to
think of them when I'm lying in bed. He makes
history seem so—well, personal, I guess. What else
do you know about the history of Saratoga?"

The girls began to walk again as Honey orga-
nized her thoughts. "Let's see," she said slowly.
"Well, the name of the town comes from an Iro-
quois Indian word that means 'place of the swift
water.' It was the swift water—the natural mineral
springs—that first turned Saratoga into a resort
town. People discovered the springs even before the
Revolutionary War, and they thought that bathing
in the water or drinking it could cure just about
any disease or ailment. Even George Washington
once came here for 'the baths,' as they were called."

Trixie giggled. "Almost every town in the East
has a hotel or a home that has a sign: WASHINGTON
SLEPT HERE. But only Saratoga can say, WASH-
INGTON BATHED HERE!"

Honey nodded, her eyes twinkling with laughter.
"Every time I think about George Washington
coming here for the baths, I picture him as he looks
on the dollar bill, with his white-powdered wig and
that stern look—only he's wearing modern-style
bathing trunks like the ones Jim and Mart and
Brian wear when we go for a swim. Isn't that an
awful way to picture the father of our country?"

Trixie was laughing so hard that she had to lean
against the building they'd been walking past. She
wrapped her arms around her body, holding her
stomach. Some of the people walking by cast worried looks in her direction, then smiled to themselves as they realized that amusement, not illness,

was the reason for her unusual posture. Honey was laughing, too, although her self-consciousness kept her from becoming as carried away as her sandy-haired friend.

Gradually Trixie regained her composure, although an occasional giggle would escape as the image of George Washington in swimming trunks again flashed through her mind.

"Oh, Honey," she gasped, "I don't know if I *dare* ask you any more questions about Saratoga. I don't think I could stand to laugh that hard again!"

The girls walked on, looking at the old and new buildings standing side by side and at the bustling crowds of people on the sidewalks and the long lines of traffic on the street.

"We should be playing the license-plate game," Trixie observed. "I've seen cars from almost every state in the East, and from many states in the Midwest and even from the West Coast."

Honey nodded. "August is the big month at Saratoga, because of the races. It's hard to believe, but for most of the year, Saratoga is a quiet little town not much bigger than Sleepyside. Then, during August, the population doubles and the excitement begins."

Trixie whistled. "I can't imagine what would happen if Sleepyside doubled in size practically overnight."

"Saratoga has been a resort town for a long, long

time," Honey reminded her. "The people here know how to handle the crowds. In fact, the town depends on them. It was a man named Gideon Putnam who started the whole thing, really. He figured out what a great attraction the mineral baths could be, so he built a hotel here and started advertising all the cures that he thought were possible from bathing in the waters, and people started coming up from New York City.

"But if you think all the cars that are here from all over the country are impressive, Trixie, imagine what Saratoga was like during the eighteen hundreds," Honey continued. "From what Daddy has told me, it seems that *everyone* who was rich and famous stayed here. Napoleon Bonaparte's brother came all the way from France to visit Saratoga!

"Back then, people really did come here as much to be seen as to see the sights. Every afternoon at three o'clock, people dressed in their fanciest clothes and went for a carriage ride down Broadway, here, or out along Union Avenue to Saratoga Lake."

Trixie closed her eyes, trying to imagine the scene. "It's fun to imagine, Honey," she said, "but I'm glad I wasn't here. All that dressing up—ugh!"

Honey smiled. "Even I would have been uncomfortable in those parades. There really was a lot of competition to see who could make the biggest splash. It wasn't just the clothes, either. Everyone tried to outdo everyone else in having the fanciest carriage pulled by the most beautiful horses. People didn't drive their own carriages, of course. They had drivers to do that, and they even tried to outdo each other in giving their drivers the fanciest uniforms to wear."

Trixie wrinkled her nose. "I think it sounds downright boring," she said. "They probably spent all morning getting into all those clothes, fixing their hair, inspecting their horses and carriages. Then they spent the afternoon sitting in the carriages, riding up and down the street—without even having the fun of driving themselves. No wonder they started going to the races. They must have been dying for something to do!"

"That must have been what John Morrisey thought," Honey said. "He was the man who brought horse racing to Saratoga. He built the first race track here back in 1863, and a year later he opened the track that we'll be going to, where the races are still held. That makes Saratoga the oldest track that's still operating in the whole country! In fact, one of the biggest stakes races here, the Travers Cup, was started in 1864, eleven years before the first Kentucky Derby!"

Once again, Trixie let out a low, appreciative whistle. "It's really incredible, Honey. We're only a hundred and fifty miles from home, and we're in a place that has so much history." She chuckled.

"Napoleon's brother and George Washington in swim trunks—practically in our backyard!"

Trixie and Honey both paused to look around them, half expecting to see the parade of fancy carriages still taking place. Instead, they noticed for the first time that, as they'd been talking, they had left the well-preserved, attractive part of Saratoga and had entered a district that had a much different feeling about it—a feeling of sadness and poverty.

The streets were lined with run-down brick and frame buildings. Hand-painted signs announced rooms for rent by the day, week, or month, and the prices told the girls that the rooms would not be like the clean, sunny one that they had just checked into. Here and there they saw a large plate glass window with the word *Restaurant* painted across it, and beyond the window, scratched wooden tables and rickety-looking chairs. Besides the cheap hotels and restaurants, many of the businesses in this neighborhood were pawnshops, their windows displaying a variety of objects that looked somehow abandoned, as though they knew that their original owners would never reclaim them.

Honey slipped her arm through Trixie's, and the girls stood close together. Looking at Honey, Trixie saw that her friend's hazel eyes were glistening with tears. *Poor Honey*, she thought. *She's so sensitive to other people's feelings. Just being here, in*

this run-down neighborhood, she's thinking about
the people who have to live here and wishing she
could do something to help them. Trixie squeezed
her friend's arm and made her own voice sound
cheerful as she said, "It's getting late. We should go
back to the hotel, before your parents start to
worry about us."

Honey nodded silently and turned back in the
direction from which they had just come. Then she
blurted, "I'm so glad I *do* have parents to worry
about me. Think about all these poor people—people who had to pawn their most prized possessions
because they had no one to turn to—" She broke off
and swallowed hard.

Not knowing what to say, Trixie squeezed
Honey's arm again, trying to remind her that she,
at least, was not alone.

"Daddy's told me about this side of Saratoga,
too," Honey said quietly. "I—I guess I never really
understood what he was talking about, though. He
says that for some people, gambling becomes a
disease. They can't stop themselves. If they're winning at the track, they tell themselves that they're
on a lucky streak. They convince themselves that
they can win a fortune if they just keep gambling,
placing bigger and bigger bets. Then when they
start to lose, they still don't stop gambling. They
tell themselves that their luck is bound to change,
and they just keep on until their winnings are all

gone. Then—" She broke off again and gestured to
the scene around them, with its cheap restaurants
and pawnshops. "They'll lose their jobs and leave
their families without a penny, just to come here
and bet everything they have on the horses."

"It's hard to believe that people could be like
that, isn't it?" Trixie asked quietly.

Honey nodded. "Daddy says that some of the
worst cases are people who work at the track. They
become so convinced that they know the horses and
can pick winners that they gamble their whole
salaries away. They never save up enough money
to get ahead—sometimes they can't even look for a
better job, because they've borrowed so much
money from their employers. Daddy says that
sometimes people like that get so desperate that,
after they pawn everything they own, they wind up
falling in with bad characters who offer to give
them money in return for helping them to fix a
race. If they're caught, they're banned from the
track, of course. But sometimes, they just take their
money and disappear, probably to go off and do
the same thing at some other track, Daddy says."

Trixie grabbed Honey's arm and spun her
around so that the two girls were face-to-face. The
anger in Trixie's eyes terrified her gentle friend.
"What are you trying to say?" Trixie demanded.

Realizing what Trixie was thinking, Honey
gasped and covered her mouth with her hand. "Oh,

no, Trixie!" she wailed. "You don't think that I—I wasn't even thinking about Regan when I said those things. Please believe me!" Tears again welled in Honey's hazel eyes, and two spilled over and slid down her cheeks.

Seeing how sincere her friend was in her denial, Trixie immediately felt ashamed of her suspicions. She put her arms around Honey and hugged her. "I'm sorry, Honey. I know you weren't thinking about Regan. But to me, as I listened to you—I don't know. It sounded almost as if you were explaining why Regan drugged Gadfly and then ran away. But it isn't true. It can't be," she concluded firmly.

The two girls walked on again in silence, sharing the same unhappy, unspoken thoughts: Both girls realized that, however much they might try to deny it, what Honey had been saying about people who worked at the track, people who were afflicted with the gambling disease, could explain Regan's running away from Saratoga seven years before. As loyal as they were to the young groom, they both had to face the fact that they didn't know very much about his past. He'd never been exactly secretive, but he hadn't spoken much about it, either. Everyone who knew him in Sleepyside had assumed that the silence was due to unhappy memories of those earlier days. But couldn't it also be due to Regan's having something to hide?

"It isn't true," Trixie repeated aloud. Even though she was starting in the middle of a thought, Honey had no trouble following it, because her thoughts had been running along such similar lines. "But even if it were," Trixie continued, "Regan's taking the job with your father would show that he was trying to get away from the gambling disease, trying to keep himself away from the track. That would mean that he really is a good person who just couldn't help the fact that he had a gambling problem."

"That's true," Honey said. "I mean, no, it isn't. I mean, that theory makes sense, but I can't believe that it's right. I just can't believe that Regan would fix a horse race, and I can't believe that he was ever a compulsive gambler, and I can't believe that—" She broke off as Trixie clutched her arm. Turning to look at her friend, she saw that Trixie's face was pale beneath its freckles and that her blue eyes were wide with horror.

"Honey, look!" Trixie breathed. "Those riding boots in the window of that pawnshop—they're Regan's!"

The Pawnshop · 8

HONEY CLOSED HER EYES for a moment, as if she were afraid of what she might see. Then her shoulders rose and fell as she took a deep breath, and she turned slowly to face the window of the pawnshop.

Even knowing what she was going to see had not prepared her for the shock, however. She was speechless for a moment, and when she did speak, her voice came out as a gasp: "Oh, Trixie, you're right!"

The girls both walked up to the window as if they were pulled by invisible strings. They stared through the window at the boots for a long, silent moment. There could be no mistake about it, they knew, although neither one of them wanted to be the first to admit it out loud.

The boots had been Regan's pride and joy. They had been handmade, especially for him, out of a soft, red brown leather. A fancy, scrollwork *R* was embossed on the top of each boot.

Honey and Trixie were both remembering, as they stood looking at the boots through the grimy window of this pawnshop in this seedy section of Saratoga, the times in the stable when they'd seen him carefully working saddle soap into the boots, removing every trace of dust and dirt, then buffing them with a soft, clean cloth until the dark leather gave off a smooth glow. They remembered, too, how often he'd told them that a pair of really good boots was as important to a rider as his saddle.

Trixie, in particular, remembered the first time Regan had told her about his feeling for good boots. She'd ridden in tennis shoes the first few times, and Regan hadn't said anything. Then, when he'd realized that Trixie was serious about becoming a good rider, he'd laid down the law: "No more riding for you, young lady, until you get some decent footgear."

"Is it really important?" Trixie had asked innocently. She'd noticed that Honey always wore special riding boots, but she'd decided that that was just due to her friend's desire to be dressed in the appropriate style for any occasion.

Regan had snorted at the question. "Do you think those little canvas things on your feet would protect them if a horse stepped on your toe?" he'd asked. "Do you think you could dig those flat rubber heels into the ground to keep a horse from running away from you when you were trying to mount him? Do you think you could kick a balky horse in the slats hard enough to get him to move, if you had to, without breaking your heels?"

Trixie had shaken her head in response to each of his questions.

"Well, then," Regan had said, "you'd better believe a good pair of boots is important." That's when he'd shown her his boots. And Trixie had volunteered for extra chores at home and worked hard to raise the money for riding boots of her own.

Remembering that conversation as if it had taken place just the day before, Trixie knew that Regan would not part with those boots without a very good reason for doing so. *And I want to know what that reason is*, she thought. Squaring her shoulders, she went to the door of the pawnshop, pushed the door open, and walked in. Honey hesitated for a moment, then followed Trixie inside.

The owner of the shop looked at them from behind a window like the teller's window of a bank. He was a fat, elderly man with a red complexion that was even redder on his large nose. His shiny bald scalp emerged from a fringe of shaggy white hair.

The startled look on the man's face said clearly that he was not used to having two young, clean-scrubbed girls walk into his shop. He looked over their heads to see if someone was following them through the door. Realizing that they were alone, he studied them curiously, without speaking.

Trixie squirmed under the old man's steady gaze. She ran through introductory speeches in her mind and quickly discarded them all. Now that she had entered the shop determined to find out how Regan's boots had come to be in the window, she realized that she could think of no way of asking for the information without arousing the owner's suspicions.

She opened her mouth to speak, closed it, cleared her throat, and turned helplessly to Honey.

As always, Honey's knack for diplomacy came to Trixie's rescue. Returning the pawnshop owner's intent look, she said in her politest voice, "Good afternoon. We were out walking, and we happened to notice the riding boots in your window. We both love to ride, and we both feel that a good pair of boots is very important to a rider. But there are so few places that carry really good riding boots these days. We were wondering if you could give us any information on where the boots in the window came from."

Inwardly, Trixie cheered her friend's little speech. Honey sounded so innocent, so calm, that no one listening would suspect that she had another reason for wanting the information from the old man. *And everything she said is true*, Trixie thought.

The shopkeeper laughed a raspy laugh that had no humor in it, even though it made his fat stomach shake. "You want to know about fancy riding boots? Then go to a fancy-riding-boot store," he said. "I run a pawnshop here, that's all. I have no idea where those boots came from, and to tell you the truth, I don't much care."

Honey's face lost its composure as she listened to the man's gruff words, and she looked as if she might turn and run out of the shop. Seeing her alarm, the man's face softened and he spoke more kindly. "Look," he said, "I make money here by taking in things that other people will want to buy. Giving somebody good money for those boots was a dumb mistake on my part. They're handmade, they're monogrammed, and they're not going to be any good to anyone but the original owner, if you know what I mean. After all these years in the business, I should know better. I *do* know better. I can listen to the saddest sob story you ever heard without turning a hair. But the guy who brought these boots in didn't tell me a sob story. He just put them down on the counter and looked me in the eye and said, 'How much?' That was all he said, but he seemed so determined, somehow, that I—"

"Who was he?" Trixie interrupted, then faltered as the shopkeeper looked at her suspiciously. "I—I mean, if we could find that man and talk to him, he might be able to tell us the name of his boot-maker," she concluded, hoping that her voice sounded as disinterested and casual as Honey's had.

The old man's suspicious look was replaced with one of amusement. "If I couldn't tell by looking that you two girls don't know much about pawn-shops, the questions you ask would sure prove it. Look, for a pawnbroker to succeed, he can't be too curious. Do you understand?" He looked from one girl to the other and saw only blank looks. He sighed.

"The people who come in here want money," he continued patiently. "They want it fast. And they want it badly enough that they're willing to take a fraction of the value of the things they bring in. Now, if these people were fine, upstanding charac-ters, they'd have other ways of putting their hands on the money. Right?" The girls nodded their agreement, and the pawnbroker continued. "I im-agine that a lot of the people who come in here have something to hide. But for me to stay healthy, I have to keep from getting curious, if you know what I mean. I don't ask questions about the names and addresses they write on their pawn tickets, even if the name is Joe Smith and the address is a rooming house that I know was torn down five years ago. I even do my best not to remember their faces. Most of the time, I give them their money and I never see them again—at least, not till the next August, when racing season starts again."

"You mean that if the man who brought in those boots came into the store right now, you wouldn't recognize him?" Trixie asked innocently.

"I didn't say that," the man replied. "I told you—that guy was different. He wasn't the usual down-and-outer that we get around here, if you know what I mean. But I don't think that finding him would do you any good, because I don't think those boots were made for him in the first place."

"Wh-Why not?" Trixie asked, her heart in her throat.

"He was a real big guy, for one thing. I didn't see his feet because I was standing behind the counter here the whole time. But unless he had *very* small feet for his size, he wouldn't have been able to cram his feet into those boots, let alone walk in them. He struck me as being a nice enough kid, but not too bright, if you know what I mean. Now, a pair of boots like that costs some money. Maybe this guy made that kind of money one time in his life, but I doubt it. He sure isn't making it now. Oh, he looked clean enough, and well fed, but he was wearing faded work clothes, and he had a homemade hair-

cut, if you know what I mean. No," the man concluded, shaking his head, "those boots weren't his.
I'd give you good odds on that."

"I—I guess he couldn't help us, then," Trixie said
abruptly. "Thank you for your time. Come on,
Honey." She turned and walked out of the shop as
quickly as she had entered it. Honey thanked the
old man and followed her back outside.

Trixie walked hurriedly for a block, shushing
Honey when she tried to speak, before she finally
slowed down and let out a long sigh. "I didn't want
to start talking things over as soon as we left the
shop, for fear the man might realize we had a
deeper interest in those boots than we'd let on," she
explained.

"I understand *that*," Honey said, "but it's about
the only thing I've heard in the past few minutes
that I do understand, Trixie. Those boots are definitely Regan's, but it just as definitely was not
Regan who left them there. What does it mean?"

Trixie shook her head. "I can't begin to figure it
out, either, Honey. But it doesn't look good. It's
hard to imagine Regan pawning those boots at all,
but if he didn't bring them in and get the money for
them. . . ." Trixie let the sentence trail off, unwilling to voice the conclusion.

"Y-You mean you think somebody stole the boots
from Regan, don't you, Trixie? And maybe hurt
him while he was doing it."

Trixie shrugged helplessly. "I don't know what I think, Honey," she admitted. "The pawnshop owner did say that the man who brought the boots in was bigger than the man they were made for. So if he decided to take the boots by force, Regan might not have been able to stop him."

"But the pawnbroker also said that he felt sorry for the man who brought the boots in, even though he's been in the business for so long that he's usually hardhearted. You know how softhearted Regan is, even though he always tries to pretend that he's not. Maybe he felt sorry for the big man, too, and gave him the boots."

"That's possible," Trixie agreed. "Especially since Regan might not want the boots himself, right now. I mean, if he's here trying to clear himself, he might not want people to know who he is. Those boots would be sure to attract attention, because they look so expensive, and they're monogrammed, besides. Oh, Honey, I hope that's it."

"Me, too," Honey said. "Anyway, that's what I'm going to believe. We have no way of knowing, yet, what really happened, so if the choice is between believing that Regan gave away his boots to someone who needed the money and believing that a crook saw the boots, thought he could get some money for them, and stole them, maybe hitting Regan over the head to get them—well, I'm just going to hope for the best, that's all." Honey nodded her head once in a "so there" gesture and looked at Trixie almost defiantly, as if she were daring her friend to contradict her.

Trixie smiled ruefully. "I'm certainly not going to argue, Honey," she said. "I want Regan to be safe as much as you do. Now, let's get back to the hotel before your parents start to worry."

"Do you think we should tell them about finding the boots?" Honey asked.

Trixie considered the question for a few minutes as they walked, then shook her head. "I don't think so, Honey. I still think that if Regan had thought your parents could help him with whatever his problem was, he would have asked for help instead of leaving the Manor House. I think he'd want us to keep this to ourselves, at least for now."

Honey nodded her agreement, although the look on her face said that she was uncomfortable about withholding the information from her parents.

The girls walked quickly out of the shabby district of Saratoga and back into the cheerful, immaculate heart of the town, both lost in thought.

Suddenly, Trixie stood still and slapped her forehead with the palm of her hand. "Gleeps!" she shouted. "How dumb can two would-be detectives get!"

"What is it, Trixie?" Honey asked. "What did you think of?"

Trixie grabbed Honey by the shoulders and looked

at her triumphantly. "Honey, don't you see? We both agreed back there that we'd try to look at the bright side of things, but we forgot the brightest side of all!" Honey stared at Trixie in bewilderment, unable to follow her best friend's train of thought.

"Don't you see?" Trixie repeated impatiently. "Up until a few minutes ago, when we saw those boots, we didn't *really* know if we were on the right track in coming to Saratoga to find Regan. Those boots prove for a fact that Regan is here—or was. And tomorrow we can really begin to look for him!"

"That Redheaded Sneak" • 9

BACK AT THE HOTEL, Honey and Trixie found a note waiting for them at the hotel desk. The note said that the Wheelers were in their room resting before dinner and that the girls should join them in the hotel dining room at seven o'clock.

"Oh, woe," Trixie sighed. "You know that I wasn't exactly overenthusiastic about going out for a fancy dinner before. And now that I know we can really start looking for Regan tomorrow morning when we go to the track, all I want to do is go to the room, pull the covers over my head, and stay there until morning."

"Not me," Honey disagreed. "Your way, it

would take ages for morning to arrive." She giggled. "Not to mention the fact that we'd be suffocated from being under all those covers by that time. I think the best thing we can do, under the circumstances, is to meet Mother and Daddy in the dining room at seven and have a perfectly perfect dinner. Then, with our stomachs so full of good food that our minds can't worry about finding Regan, we can come back to our room and fall right to sleep."

"You're right, Honey," Trixie admitted. "We did come to Saratoga for a vacation, after all, so we might as well enjoy ourselves. I'm sure I will enjoy myself, too, once the dinner gets started."

"Goodness!" Honey exclaimed as she glanced at the clock above the desk. "Dinner gets started in less than an hour! We'd better get up to the room right away, so we'll both have plenty of time to shower, dry our hair, and change clothes!"

Forty-five minutes later, Honey was ready to go, her hair brushed and shining, her white pleated skirt and lime green top looking crisp and cool. Trixie was standing in front of the mirror, looking critically at her reflection. She was wearing a gingham sundress, but the navy pantsuit that was lying on her bed was evidence that the dress hadn't been her first choice.

"I think you look fine, Trixie," Honey said.

"I don't know, Honey," Trixie said. "It still seems too casual, compared to what you're wearing, even though it *is* a dress. The pantsuit really seems dressier, but that's pants, and— Oh, never mind. Let's just go downstairs. It's so dark in that restaurant that nobody will be able to see what I'm wearing, anyway." Turning resolutely away from the mirror, she snatched the pantsuit off the bed, put it on a hanger, and hung it in the closet.

Honey took Trixie's place in front of the mirror, smoothing her skirt and giving her hair one more sweep with the brush. Trixie stood behind her and looked at their reflections in the mirror. Her eyes moved from Honey's hazel eyes, smooth blond hair, and slender body to her own curly hair, snub nose, and stocky figure. Then she crossed her eyes, wrinkled her nose, and stuck her tongue out. As Honey burst out laughing, Trixie let her face relax in a smile. "See?" she said. "No matter how funny I look ordinarily, it's nice to know that I can look even funnier if I really try."

"You're not funny-looking, Trixie," Honey protested. "You're very nice-looking. If you don't believe me, you should hear what Jim said about you right before he left for camp."

"What did he say?" Trixie demanded. "No, don't tell me." She covered her ears with her hands and closed her eyes. Then, realizing that she was overreacting, she lowered her hands, opened her eyes, and repeated nonchalantly, "What did he say?"

"What he said," Honey drawled slowly, knowing that her friend was itching with impatience, "what he said," she repeated, "was, 'As pretty as Trixie has been getting lately, I'm almost afraid to leave for camp for three weeks. When I come back, she'll probably be the belle of Sleepyside, with so many boyfriends lined up that she won't have time for old friends!'"

Trixie blushed violently. "Jim didn't say that," she said. "Even if he did, he was just teasing. He couldn't have meant it."

"I don't think Jim really meant that you wouldn't have time for him," Honey agreed. "He knows you're too loyal a friend to let that happen. I *do* think he was being perfectly serious about how pretty you're getting, though."

Trixie looked at her blushing face in the mirror and sighed. "Right now, I must admit that I have an all-American look, Honey: blue eyes, white teeth, and bright red face! Let's go, before you make me so embarrassed that I go back to my original plan and spend the rest of the night hidden under the covers!"

Laughing, Honey picked up her purse and followed Trixie to the door. Pausing in the doorway, Honey suddenly turned serious, and she reached out and put her hand on Trixie's arm. "Before we go downstairs," she said, "I just want to ask you one more time: Do you still feel that we should keep the fact that we found Regan's boots a secret from Mother and Daddy?''

"Do you want to tell them, Honey?" Trixie asked.

"I don't know," Honey said, shrugging. "What you said before is true. A lot of people looking for Regan while he's trying to stay hidden could drive him away. I just hate to think that he could need food or money, or even a doctor, and not be able to get what he needs until we find him—if we find him."

Trixie looked solemn, and she was silent for a moment as she thought over what Honey had said. Finally she shook her head. "We have to keep the secret a little longer, Honey. I don't know why I feel that way, because everything you say is true. But I just think keeping quiet about the boots is the right thing to do." She forced herself to look directly into Honey's worried hazel eyes, hoping she was projecting a confidence that she didn't entirely feel.

"Let's go to dinner," Honey said, replacing her worried look with a cheerful smile. "We're on vacation, after all!"

The girls were subdued when they entered the dining room and took their places at the candlelit table where Honey's parents were already sitting. After the girls assured Mr. and Mrs. Wheeler that the drive up from Sleepyside had been a pleasant one and that they had enjoyed their walk around

Saratoga that afternoon, conversation ceased as everyone studied the huge, leather-covered menus.

"Do you girls know what you'd like?" Mrs. Wheeler asked after a few moments.

Trixie giggled. "It takes me a long time to get through a menu like this, Mrs. Wheeler, because I have to read all the descriptions of the dishes; none of them are things I'm familiar with. Even so, instead of one of the fancy dishes with French names, what I'd like is prime rib. It's something I don't get at home, where there are six mouths to feed."

"I'm in the mood for fish, so I'll have the red snapper," Honey said.

"Fine," Mr. Wheeler said, beckoning to the waiter. "Your mother and I decided this afternoon that we were both hungry for lobster, so I guess we're ready to order." He gave the waiter their orders, then turned back to the girls. "I think you'll both enjoy the plans I've made for tomorrow, if you don't mind getting out of bed at the crack of dawn."

"The earlier we get started, the more we'll be able to see," Trixie told him.

"That's exactly what I thought," Mr. Wheeler said. "So I've arranged for the three of us to attend the workouts at the track tomorrow morning, while my wife indulges her love of shopping. It's something that most visitors to Saratoga don't get to see, because the security restrictions at the track are pretty tight. But Mr. Worthington was able to get clearance for us, so you'll get to see the horses and jockeys working out in the morning and then watch them race in the afternoon."

"That sounds super, Mr. Wheeler. I hope you'll thank Mr. Worthington for us," Trixie said.

"Oh, you'll be able to do that yourself," he assured her. "Mr. Worthington will be at the workout tomorrow morning; he has horses racing at Saratoga this week."

"I was hoping I'd get a chance to ask him some questions," Trixie blurted. "I—I mean, to ask someone some questions about horse racing," she finished lamely.

Mr. Wheeler didn't seem to notice Trixie's near slip of the tongue. "Mr. Worthington would be a good person to talk to about racing," he told her. "He's been racing horses at the finest tracks in the country for a number of years."

At least seven years, anyway, Trixie thought, *because that's when Regan worked for him. I wonder if I'll be able to find out anything from talking to him.*

Trixie was so lost in thought that she didn't even notice the waiter standing beside her, holding the tray of food. When Honey called her name across the table, Trixie started, then blushed and stammered, "I—I'm sorry. I was thinking about—about the track."

Mrs. Wheeler laughed. "It's a true horse lover who'd rather think about horses than eat, Trixie."

Trixie looked at the huge slab of beautifully cooked, lean, pink meat on her plate and at the baked potato topped with sour cream and a sprinkling of finely cut chives. "Then I guess I'm not a true horse lover," she said ruefully, "because now that I've seen this food, I'd much rather eat!"

"Me, too!" Honey agreed enthusiastically. "I didn't realize it until I saw the food, but I'm starved!"

The two girls turned their total attention to their food, trading portions of fish and prime rib and sampling some of the lobsters that the Wheelers skillfully extracted from the shell and gave to them.

After dinner, the girls left Mr. and Mrs. Wheeler to enjoy their coffee while they went to their room for a good night's sleep before their early wake-up call. Honey fell asleep almost immediately, but Trixie stared at the ceiling, trying to decide if she'd done the right thing in persuading Honey to hide their new evidence from her parents. *I'd rather face a gang of crooks with their guns drawn than have to decide what's best for someone else*, she thought. *What if Regan does need help—needs it right now—and my decision keeps him from getting it?*

"Well, right or wrong, the decision has been made," she murmured finally. "I'll just have to live with it until something happens to change my mind." Then she rolled over and went to sleep.

The two girls were sleepy-eyed the next morning as they dressed, met Mr. Wheeler in the lobby, and rode with him to the track, but the excitement of the workouts soon had them wide-awake.

"This is like a sixty-two-ring circus!" Trixie exclaimed as she tried to get her bearings in the bustle of activity.

Mr. Worthington, who had been on hand to greet them and was now standing with them near the fence that bordered the track, chuckled at Trixie's amazement. "It is that," he agreed. "You see, Trixie, these workouts are extremely important for many reasons. They limber up the horses, helping to prevent injuries during the races. They give the horse and jockey a chance to get to know each other. They also give the trainers a chance to detect injuries that mean the horse shouldn't be run that afternoon. But those of us who have a stake in the outcome of the day's races view these workouts as a necessary evil, at best."

"Evil?" Trixie questioned. "With everything you've just said, the workouts sound like a good idea to me."

"There's another side to the workouts, too," Mr. Worthington continued. "They provide an opportunity for other trainers and owners to see all the horses before they race. They provide an opportunity for the timers who work for the racing sheets to time the horses and publish the workout times the same day, which can affect the betting on a race. In short, they lessen the element of surprise, which is vital in racing. That's why there's such a hubbub at the track during the workouts: Everyone is trying to give his horse a good warm-up without giving away any information."

"I'm afraid I don't understand how the need for secrecy creates so much activity," Honey said. "I mean, I always think of secrecy as being something—well, *quiet*. It certainly isn't quiet here," she concluded, looking around her.

"The best way to explain is to show you some examples," Mr. Worthington said. "Example number one. Do you see that chestnut horse down at the turn? His jockey is walking him quietly, as though he had nothing on his mind but a leisurely ride. But do you see those two men over there, who seem to be absorbed in conversation? They're the owner and the trainer of that horse. Now, I'll make a prediction. When the horse rounds the turn, the jockey will suddenly urge him into a full gallop, the men's conversation will cease, and they'll each pull a stopwatch out of their pocket. The jockey will run the horse for a half-mile, the owner and trainer will have a time on him, and if they're lucky, their little game will have worked and no one else will have seen what they were doing in time to clock the horse."

Trixie and Honey both looked at the horse and

rider, then at the two men Mr. Worthington had pointed out, then looked back at their host as if they were a little worried about his sanity. The two men were completely absorbed in their conversation, not even glancing at the horse; and the jockey was slouching in the saddle as if he were not even aware that he was riding. Mr. Worthington, sensing their disbelief, just smiled and signaled to the two girls to pay attention as the horse came round the turn.

Suddenly, the horse burst into a run and Mr. Worthington's prediction came true before the two girls' startled eyes. They watched, awestruck, as the horse completed the half-mile run. Glancing over at the two men, the girls saw them checking their stopwatches. When the girls turned back to Mr. Worthington, they chuckled as they saw that he, too, had pulled out a stopwatch and was now calculating the horse's time. "It was only an average run," he said with exaggerated calm, enjoying the astonishment he had created in his two young guests. "It's really much more exciting when you manage to see through the charade and clock a horse that you realize is going to be a sure thing in his race that afternoon."

Trixie grinned up at Mr. Worthington. "If you're apologizing for not providing more excitement, please don't bother. I think my heart missed about three beats when that horse broke into a gallop."

"The two men who know all the games that go
on at the track are sitting on the fence over there,"
Mr. Worthington said, pointing to two men Trixie
hadn't noticed before. "They're the timers for the
racing sheets. You'll notice that each of them is
holding *two* stopwatches and a thick book. The
book is full of Thoroughbred registration forms,
because we owners are so secretive that we'll even
try to keep a new horse's identity a secret during his
first workout. Those two men are such experts at
playing our games that they can time two horses
running two different stretches of track while
discussing the possible identity of a strange horse—
all at the same time!"

Trixie and Honey found this new piece of information impossible to believe, but after what
they'd just seen, they were afraid *not* to believe Mr.
Worthington. They moved closer to the two timers,
and they were soon spellbound by the rapid chatter
that they heard between the two men.

"That chestnut gelding over there is new. Got a
line on him? Could be the new South American
horse that's running out of Carleton Farms now. I
got one-forty-eight for the half on that bay over
there. Could be holding back or just good to run
out of the money."

"Rumor is his shoulder's gone bad. Could be real
time or just a little joke on us so he can open up this
afternoon and take the money. The chestnut can't

be the new Carleton horse. The book shows a blaze
on the forehead of that one. Better ask around after
the workout."

"I can hardly understand a thing they're talking
about, Honey. Can you?" Trixie asked.

Honey shook her head. "They seem to understand each other, though, Trixie. And here I
thought you and I were the only two people in the
world who could talk gibberish and still understand each other perfectly!"

Laughing, the two girls turned their attention
back to the timers and listened and watched until
the crowd began to thin and the workout ended.

"That was super!" Trixie said when she and
Honey rejoined Mr. Worthington and Mr. Wheeler.
"Thank you so much for inviting us here!"

"That look of excitement on your face is all the
thanks I need," Mr. Worthington replied. "I've
devoted a lot of my time and money to racing. It's
good to see someone else catching the spirit that I
feel. If you want to reward me, though, there is
something you can do."

"Anything!" the girls chorused.

"Well, then, come back to the stables with me
and let me show off my horses," Mr. Worthington
said, his eyes twinkling.

"It does seem like the least we can do for Mr.
Worthington, doesn't it, Honey?" Trixie said, falling in with the joke.

"Oh, certainly," Honey said. "I didn't really want to visit the stables and see all those beautiful Thoroughbreds up close and learn more about racing, but I wouldn't want to be impolite."

With exaggerated dignity, the two girls linked arms and followed the adults to the stables. Once they were around the horses, however, their pose dissolved, and they found themselves *ooh*ing and *aah*ing at the beautiful animals that were being groomed and curried in preparation for the afternoon's racing.

In one stall, a small, weathered man was working over a sleek, glistening horse.

"Carl," Mr. Worthington said to the man, "we have guests. Trixie Belden and Honey Wheeler, meet my trainer, Carl Stinson. Carl has been with Worthington Farms for over twenty years."

Trixie and Honey exchanged an electrified glance as they realized that this was the man that Regan had worked for.

"How d'you do?" Carl Stinson asked curtly, returning his attention to the horse.

"Do you mind if we watch you for a while?" Honey asked.

"Nope," the trainer replied, not bothering to look up.

"That's a good idea," Mr. Worthington said. "I have some business to discuss with Mr. Wheeler, and I'm sure you girls will be more interested in learning about Carl's horse sense than about our dollars and cents. We'll meet you back here in a few minutes."

"That sounds great, Mr. Worthington," Trixie said, "if Mr. Stinson doesn't mind."

"Carl won't mind, as long as you stay out of his way and don't frighten the horses. Right, Carl?" Mr. Worthington asked.

"Right," the trainer replied, still not looking up from his minute inspection of the beautiful Thoroughbred.

Mr. Worthington and Mr. Wheeler walked away, quickly lost in conversation, and the girls stood quiet, watching the trainer.

Carl Stinson finished his inspection of the horse and began rubbing him down with liniment. Then he buckled ice packs around the horse's front knees.

"What are those for?" Trixie asked.

"Keeps the swelling down," Stinson replied.

Trixie gave Honey an anguished glance. This man could provide important information about Regan, but only if they could get him to talk, and it was beginning to seem as if that might be an impossibility.

"This is one of the most beautiful Thoroughbreds I've ever seen, Mr. Stinson. You must be very proud of him."

Stinson paused in his work and gave Honey a sidelong glance. "More than proud, miss. There's a big chunk of my life invested in this horse. Name's Gadbox, son of Gadfly out of Jack-In-The-Box.''

The girls stood in startled silence, which the trainer mistook for confusion. "That means his father was a horse named Gadfly and his mother was named Jack-In-The-Box," he explained. "Gadfly was the best horse I ever trained. Pegged him as a winner first time I ever saw him work out. When we had to retire him, I thought I'd never see his like again. And I didn't, for five long, dry years. Then, two years ago, he presented me with Gadbox, here, and I knew I had another winner.'' Stinson stopped speaking suddenly. He stood with his mouth clamped shut, the muscles in his jaw moving as he gritted his teeth.

The girls stood silent, too, moved by the depth of emotion they sensed behind the trainer's brief speech. Both knew that he hadn't really been speaking to them at all, but to himself, remembering his hopes for Gadbox, the son of the horse he'd pegged for a winner. *No wonder he says there's a chunk of his life invested in Gadbox*, Trixie thought.

Carl Stinson reached out and began to stroke Gadbox's silky neck. "I'm not going to make the same mistake twice," he said intensely. "I'm not going to trust anyone else with this horse. No one touches him, grooms him, or feeds him but me. His sire could have gone all the way, become one of the greatest horses in history. Now his son has a chance, and no thieving little groom like that Regan kid is going to dope him before a big race and ruin his chances." The trainer's face had hardened as he spoke, and when he spoke Regan's name, his mouth twisted as though the word had left a bitter taste.

Trixie felt tears welling in her eyes. It was painful to hear this stranger speaking of Regan, her good friend, with such contempt. She wanted to blurt out a defense. "Regan—" she began, then stopped when she felt Honey's hand on her arm.

The trainer turned and looked at her. "Yes, Regan," he said. "He was a groom who worked for me seven years ago. He wasn't more than sixteen when he came to me looking for a job. A runaway. From what, I don't know. Didn't ask. Just took him in. Treated him like a son. Taught him about horses. And he learned fast. He had a natural gift for working with horses, that boy. So I started trusting him with more and more of the work around here. Thought he'd be able to take over from me someday." Stinson snorted. "But someday wasn't good enough for that redheaded sneak. He had no time for living on a groom's wages and taking orders from me. So he found a way to make some fast money by doping a horse. He ruined Gadfly, and he almost ruined me. But not quite. Not quite." Abruptly, the trainer straightened his stooped shoulders and turned to face the girls.

"You better move along," he said. "I have to feed Gadbox before the racing starts, and I don't even let anybody see where I keep his feed. Not anymore."

The girls stood in confused silence for a moment after the trainer finished speaking. His attack on Regan had left them shaken, unable to move. Then they heard the voices of Mr. Worthington and Honey's father as the two men neared Gadbox's stall. Trixie pulled herself together, taking a deep breath to try to ease the tightness in her chest.

Honey once again put her hand on Trixie's arm, pulling her friend in the direction of Mr. Worthington's voice. "I hope Gadbox does as well as you hope, Mr. Stinson," she said in a soft, trembling voice.

A moment later, Mr. Worthington's booming voice shattered the stillness. "Come along, girls," he said. "We have to have a bite to eat and then get to our seats before the racing starts."

At the Races • 10

HONEY AND TRIXIE walked miserably along behind
Mr. Wheeler and their host. *It can't be true*, Trixie
thought, *it just can't*. Turning to look at Honey, she
saw her own misery reflected in her friend's eyes.
More than anything, she wanted to be alone with
Honey, to talk over what Carl Stinson had said and
to refute, out loud, the accusations that he had
made. But there was no opportunity for the girls to
be alone during lunch, so Trixie was forced to keep
her jumbled thoughts to herself.

Part of her misery, she knew, came from not being able to discount everything that the trainer had
said. Regan had always been very loyal to all his

friends. But he was also a strongly independent man whose fiery temper matched his hair. It was very easy for her to imagine Regan's growing impatience at taking curtly worded orders from the trainer and his feeling of helplessness at the thought that it would be years before he would be given full responsibility for the horses he was working on. Still, that wouldn't mean that he'd have had to dope a horse. He could have just left, found a better job somewhere else. Unless—

Unless, Trixie thought, *unless he had gambling debts to clear up before he left. If he were in debt, that might have seemed like the only way to pay them off so that he could leave without being followed.* She bit her lower lip, hard, to chase the thought from her mind. The real pain of her teeth digging into her own lip was better than the emotional pain she felt when she found herself doubting Regan's innocence.

"Is anything wrong, Trixie?" Mr. Worthington asked.

Trixie shook her head. "I have a little bit of a headache," she told him. "I guess there was just too much excitement this morning."

"I understand," Mr. Worthington said. "But I'm sorry you're not feeling good. You've hardly touched your hamburger. Why don't you try to finish it? It might be just what you need to perk yourself up and get back in the spirit of things."

"I'll try," Trixie said, smiling across the table at Mr. Worthington.

"By the way, what did you think of Carl Stinson?" Mr. Worthington asked.

"He seems like a very knowledgeable person," Honey replied.

Mr. Worthington laughed. "That probably means that he hardly spoke to you the whole time you were with him. Carl isn't much for talk, but he's the best man with horses I've ever seen. I'm lucky to have him working with me. I trust Carl so completely that I can leave all the details of running the stables to him, and just concern myself with the buying and selling end of the business—and the excitement of watching the horses race, of course."

"What kinds of details does Mr. Stinson handle?" Trixie asked.

"You'd be surprised how many there are," Mr. Worthington said. "Of course, the main work of a trainer is training the horses—deciding whether they need tough workouts to make them give everything they have or light workouts to keep them from losing their speed and endurance before the race, for example. Some trainers don't do much more than that. But Carl does much, much more. He makes sure that the horses are moved from track to track in the most efficient way possible, in terms of both saving money and saving wear and tear on the horses. He decides what food they should have, and he finds out where to get it at the best price. And, of course, he's responsible for the rest of the staff. He makes all decisions on hiring and firing grooms and exercise people, putting on extra help when we need it and laying people off when we don't. All I do is give him a budget. He decides how to use it. Why, right now I couldn't even tell you how many people are working for Worthington Farms, let alone who they are or where they came from."

"Has it always been that way?" Honey asked.

"Oh, not at first, of course," Mr. Worthington replied. "But remember, Carl has been with me for twenty years. All of these responsibilities fell to him gradually. I'd say that he's been fully in charge for the past fifteen years or so."

Trixie looked at Honey and raised her eyebrows. That let Mr. Worthington out as a source of information about Regan. The two had probably never even met.

"Actually," Mr. Worthington continued, "when I said I was lucky to have Carl working for me, I wasn't being exactly accurate. Truthfully, I have Carl working for me because I'm unlucky." He chuckled at the girls' bewildered looks. "What I mean is that we haven't been very lucky with our horses the past few years. The stable has just about broken even; we haven't actually lost money, but we haven't made any, either. And that, in a way, is what's kept Carl with me. He'd like to be an owner himself, and he has all the knowledge of both training and finances to do it. But, although he's paid a fair salary, he needs the bonus he'd get for bringing along a real winning horse to raise the capital to buy stock and set himself up in business. So you see," Mr. Worthington concluded, "if my luck improves and I have one or two good seasons, I'll probably lose my trainer."

"Does that mean you'd rather not win?" Trixie asked bluntly.

Mr. Worthington scowled, and for a moment Trixie was afraid that he was about to lose his temper. Then he regained control and chuckled once again. "Of course not," he said. "Carl is a brilliant trainer, but no one is irreplaceable. I've devoted my life to making money because I like making money. The horses have been pretty much a hobby until now, but if they turned into a profitable concern, I'd be as pleased as anyone. And now I'd suggest that we take our seats at the track. The race will be starting soon."

Mrs. Wheeler joined them in Mr. Worthington's private box at the track, chatting happily about her morning's shopping and asking the girls about their behind-the-scenes tour. The girls assured her that the morning had been very educational, exchang-

ing a guilty glance as they both thought again
about how much of the reason for their trip to
Saratoga they were keeping secret from Honey's
parents.

"With what you learned this morning, you
should be well able to make some educated picks
this afternoon," Mr. Wheeler said jovially. "If you
have any sure things you'd like to tell me about, I'll
be happy to listen."

"I'd say Gadbox is a sure thing," Trixie said.
"And I'd say nobody should bet on that bay we saw
this morning."

"The bay is in the first race," Mr. Worthington
said. "There are only four horses in the race, so if
you've eliminated one of them, you only have three
left to pick from. Which one do you like?" He
handed her his copy of the racing form, which con-
tained information about all of the horses that
would be racing that day.

Trixie and Honey studied it carefully, trying to
make sense of the mass of information about the
horses' sires and dams, their workout times from
that morning, and their record of wins and losses in
past races.

Finally Trixie handed the form back to Mr.
Worthington with a sigh. "I guess my favorite
horse for the first race is Freckles. That isn't based
on his track record, his workout time, or his
breeding record."

"I know what it's based on," Honey said with a giggle. "The reason for your choice is as clear as the nose on your face—or maybe I should say as clear as the freckles on the nose on your face."

"You guessed it, Honey," Trixie said. "If that poor horse has freckles, too, he has my sympathy—and my hopes for his good luck."

"I'll pretend that I went down to the window and placed a bet on him for you," Mr. Wheeler said, laughing.

Very soon, the horses were being led onto the track. "That has to be Freckles," Trixie said, pointing to a dapple gray horse that stood out against the field of bays and chestnuts.

"It is indeed," Mr. Worthington said after he'd checked the horse's number against his racing form. "And the horse we saw this morning in the workout is number five, Willmore. We'll soon see if his time this morning was his all-out best or if we were fooled by his trainer's little game."

The horses were settled in their gates, the gun went off, and the race began. Freckles took an early lead, then began to lose ground to the other horses. At the same time, Willmore began to move up, and at the finish line he was in the lead by more than a length, while Freckles lagged far behind.

Trixie tossed both hands into the air. "So much for all the inside information I picked up this morning," she said, with a bleak smile.

Mrs. Wheeler hugged her. "It happens to the best of them, Trixie," she said. "Real gamblers don't let it keep them from trying again."

Trixie and Honey did try again—and again. But in the first three races, they found themselves out of the "pretend" money every time.

The fourth race was the one that Gadbox was entered in. "Here's your sure thing, Trixie. Do you want me to increase the size of your 'bet'?" Mr. Wheeler asked.

"It isn't as though you've lost a small fortune, Trixie," Mrs. Wheeler said reassuringly. "We wanted you to have a good time at the races, and part of having a good time is betting, especially when it's 'pretend' betting, which doesn't hurt, even when you lose!"

"Well-l-l," Trixie said slowly, going along with the game and acting as if she wanted to be persuaded.

"Come on, Trixie, let's have a sort of bet," Honey urged. "Think how bad Gadbox would feel if he found out his two new friends didn't even bet on him!"

At Honey's words, a picture formed in Trixie's mind of the beautiful Thoroughbred pouting in his stall, his lower lip stuck out like that of a hurt child. She began to giggle so hard that she could only nod her agreement to Mr. Wheeler.

Mr. Worthington and his guests all leaped to their feet the minute the gun signaled the start of the fourth race, and all of them strained nearly as hard as their favorite horse for the duration of the race. The girls jumped up and down and screamed until their voices broke. The adults, trying to be more dignified, lost their composure, and they, too, began to shout encouragement as the horses came round the final turn and Gadbox began to surge into the lead.

When he finally crossed the finish line, he was four lengths ahead of the second-place horse. Trixie and Honey threw their arms around each other, dancing up and down with excitement.

"We finally picked a winner, Trixie!" Honey said.

At Honey's words, Trixie's elation vanished. "That's right, Honey," she said soberly. "We finally picked a winner. And in the excitement I forgot that, if we were really playing horses, I'd picked three losers before, and I hadn't paid for the winning ticket, either. I also forgot how much of my 'winnings' should go to pay back the money lent me."

Smiling, Mr. Wheeler said, "I very much admire your honesty, young lady."

Trixie flushed at his praise and pretended to study the racing sheet in order to cover her embarrassment. Suddenly she was struck by an alarming thought: With twelve imaginary dollars in her hands from her winning imaginary bet, Trixie had

completely forgotten even Mr. Wheeler's generosity in buying her dinner the night before and lunch
just that afternoon, to say nothing of the hotel bill.
Everything had fled from her mind at the thought
of having even twelve extra *imaginary* dollars to
spend as she pleased. And for her, they would have
been *extra* dollars, not needed for food or a roof
over her head. What if she were really poor, and
what if there were a lot more than twelve dollars at
stake? It would be even easier, under those circumstances, to forget about loyalty, to forget about
someone who had treated you well. *Is that what
happened to Regan seven years ago?* Trixie
thought. Try as she might, she couldn't get the
bothersome idea out of her mind. She turned it over
and over again during the rest of the afternoon.
Once again she wished that she could get Honey
alone so that the two girls could talk, but it wasn't
possible. Even when Trixie suggested that she and
Honey go to the refreshment stand for a soft drink,
Mrs. Wheeler decided to come along to stretch her
legs.

Worried and distracted, Trixie found it hard to
keep her hosts from realizing that she was no
longer enjoying herself at the races. She was relieved when the last race was over and the stands
began to clear.

"Shall we go down to the winners' circle?" Mr.
Wheeler asked.

"I—I'd rather not," Trixie said. "It's been such a long day. I'd like to go back to the hotel and rest for a while."

"Don't tell me Trixie Belden finally ran out of energy!" Mr. Wheeler teased. "I could have made a fortune taking bets that that would never happen!"

"Now, Matthew," Mrs. Wheeler said, "don't try to change her mind. Let's send the girls back to the hotel in a taxi. We can meet them there in a couple of hours and go out on the town for dinner. That'll give them a chance to freshen up a little."

"Thanks, Mrs. Wheeler," Trixie said gratefully. "I'll see you at the hotel. Thank you, too, for showing us around, Mr. Worthington."

Honey, looking vaguely worried at her best friend's strangely quiet mood, thanked Mr. Worthington and followed Trixie out of the stands.

The two girls walked slowly through the rapidly thinning crowd to the front gate of the racetrack, where a row of taxis was waiting to pick up passengers returning to their homes and hotels.

Suddenly Trixie broke into a run, weaving through the crowd and shouting, "Excuse me, please!" as she pushed her way past startled adults. Honey followed, trying to keep Trixie in sight without knocking anyone out of the way.

When they were almost at the front gate, Trixie stopped running as abruptly as she had begun. "Wh-What is going on, Trixie?" Honey asked breathlessly as she came up beside her friend.

"Oh, Honey," Trixie wailed, "I saw a redheaded man in the crowd. I tried to catch up to him, but he just disappeared!"

Supersleuth Honey • 11

HONEY STARED at her friend open-mouthed for a moment, then closed her mouth and swallowed hard. "Oh, Trixie," she said, her voice cracking, "do you think it was Regan?"

Trixie's mouth turned down at the corners and she shrugged. "I don't know, Honey. I never got close enough to him to tell for sure. The man I saw was about the right size, and he had red hair. That's all I know."

"Oh!" Honey exclaimed in disgust, stamping her foot. "This whole day has been one frustration after another. I've felt as though I were about to explode, having to keep all my feelings to myself because you and I were never alone to talk things over."

"That's exactly how I've felt, Honey," Trixie said. "That's why I passed up the chance to go to the winners' circle, much as I'd like to any other time. Now we have a couple of hours to talk things over before your parents get to the hotel, starting as soon as we can catch a cab."

Unfortunately, the girls' chance to talk was postponed by their cabdriver, an outgoing, chatty man who began a one-sided conversation almost as soon as the girls got into the cab.

"It sure is nice to have a couple of fresh-faced young ladies in the cab for a change," he said. "The customers who usually climb into this hack at the track are a different-looking bunch. High rollers and down-and-outers, but all of 'em people who've been around the track too long. Yessir, you ladies are a nice change of pace. Boy, you should have seen the last guy I drove back to town. Now that was a tough customer if ever I saw one, and I've seen my share. This guy was big and mean-looking. Nasty scar running all down one side of his face, like he'd got on the wrong end of a knife fight sometime in his life."

"I saw that man, too, when we were at the concession stand at the track," Trixie said.

"Then you know what I'm talking about," the driver said, barely stopping his flow of chatter long enough to absorb Trixie's observation. "Yessir, I've seen 'em all. I've driven guys to the track who were laughin' and jokin' with me all the way out, and picked those same guys up a couple of hours later lookin' like they were about to bust out cryin'. And I've seen guys lookin' like the cat that ate the canary after a good day's bettin', and I've seen guys who looked like they'd never lose at the track 'cause they'd do whatever they had to to see that their horses won.

"Some of the ladies are somethin' else, too. I get little old ladies that look like they should be home sittin' in a rockin' chair on the front porch and tendin' to their knittin', unless you look close enough to see the gleam in their eye that means they're all set to wager a bundle on the ponies. And I get ladies who are all dolled up like they're goin' to meet the queen of England, with so much perfume on it makes my eyes water. The saddest, though, are the gamblers' wives. They come along with their husbands to the track because they think maybe they can stop them from losing their shirts, but they know in their hearts that they can't. So they just sit in the backseat all quiet and tense, chewin' their lips and lookin' half scared to death." The cabbie shook his head. "They're the ones I feel sorry for. I try to laugh and joke with 'em to make 'em feel better, but it doesn't work. I always want to say, 'Hey, you can't do any good comin' out here

with your man and sufferin' while you watch him
lose the rent money. Why don't you just wait at
home, watch TV or read a book and try to take
your mind off the inevitable?' I always want to say
that, but I never do. Probably wouldn't do any
good, anyway." The cabbie shook his head again.

"Excuse me," Honey said quickly as the cabbie
paused briefly in his nonstop chatter, "you see so
many people here, I was wondering if you could
answer a question for me. I've been wondering all
day if there's some kind of superstition about
redheads causing bad luck at the racetrack, or
something. It seems as though I didn't see a single
redhead all day. You see, my brother is a redhead,
so I'm very conscious of them, and that's what
made me think of it."

The cabbie chuckled. "There's no superstition
about redheads at the track that I know of, and I
know 'em all: rabbits' feet and horseshoes over the
barn doors and lucky shirts and lucky rings and
lucky days of the week. Nope, I'd say there are
probably just fewer redheads in the world than you
think there are, since your brother's a redhead.

"Matter of fact," the cabbie continued, "I had a
guy with bright red hair in the cab just this morning. Nice-looking young fellow he was, and real
polite, even though he did smell to high heaven of
horses. He apologized for it, which is more than
those ladies with their heavy perfume ever do, even

though I'd rather have the smell of horses in my cab any day than all those exotic concoctions. At least he came by his horse perfume honestly, since he works at a boarding stable around here, I found out. Yessir, he was a real nice young guy, and a redhead to boot."

The cabbie continued his conversation with himself, but the girls were beyond listening to him. Trixie grabbed Honey's hand and held it hard to keep from shrieking in her excitement. From the pressure Trixie felt from Honey's hand, she knew that her usually quiet friend was having just as much trouble trying to keep her excitement in check.

The minute the cabbie stopped in front of their hotel, the girls paid him, thanked him for the ride, and raced through the lobby and up to their room. Sitting cross-legged on one of the large double beds, they began to discuss the events of the day.

"I just know it was Regan that the cabbie took to the track this morning," Honey said.

Trixie nodded. "And I'm sure, now, that it was Regan I chased through the crowd at the track. Drat! I wish I'd been able to catch up with him. Then our search would already be over, and we'd have the entire story by now. But we're so close, Honey! There can't be that many boarding stables around, even in a horse town like Saratoga. I'll bet anything that by this time tomorrow, we'll have found Regan. And it's all thanks to you, Honey, for playing your hunch and asking the cabbie about redheads at the track. I'll have to start calling you 'Supersleuth Honey'!"

To Trixie's astonishment, Honey suddenly burst into tears. "What is it, Honey? What's wrong? You should be thrilled! Our search for Regan is almost over!"

Honey's response was to cry even harder. She threw herself onto the bed, burying her face in one of the pillows, her shoulders heaving as she sobbed.

Trixie was becoming really frightened. Her best friend was, she knew, a very sensitive and, sometimes, highly emotional person, quick to feel both joy and sadness. But never before had Honey reacted with such intensity—and with so little warning. Trixie was at a loss to know what to do. Finally she went into the bathroom and pulled some tissues out of the dispenser on the wall and took them in to Honey, who took them wordlessly, still crying too hard even to say, "Thank you."

Then Trixie sat on the other bed and watched and waited until her friend's sobbing diminished. When it had almost stopped, Trixie got up and went into the bathroom again, returning with a washcloth that she had wrung out of cold water. When she returned to the bedroom, Honey had rolled over to lie on her back. She was staring at the ceiling, her chin trembling from the effort she was making to hold back her tears.

Trixie held the washcloth out to her. "Fold this up and put it over your eyes," she instructed her friend. "That'll keep your eyes from getting swollen."

Honey nodded, still unable to speak, then took the cloth and put it over her eyes. Trixie sat down again and waited quietly for a few more minutes. "Do you think you can talk about it now?" she asked finally.

Honey nodded, pulled the cloth off her eyes, sat up on the bed, and blew her nose loudly. "I was so excited when the cabdriver told us about giving a ride to the redheaded man. But then, as you started talking about how close we are to finding Regan, I suddenly felt really terrified. A voice in the back of my mind screamed, 'I don't want to find him!' And then I felt guilty and frightened and confused, all at the same time, and I—" Honey's voice broke, and she swallowed hard and blew her nose again, then sat silent, staring down at her hands.

"I think I understand," Trixie said quietly. "I had some of the same feelings today, after we talked to Carl Stinson."

"Trixie, I wouldn't say this to another soul in the whole world, but I—I really have a hard time keeping faith in Regan's innocence. Carl Stinson must be an honest person—Mr. Worthington wouldn't have kept him on as a trainer and given him so much responsibility if he weren't. And Carl Stinson really believes that Regan is guilty. The Regan that we've always known is completely trustworthy. I'd trust him with my life. But the fact is that *somebody* gave drugs to Gadfly seven years ago. And we don't know what Regan was like seven years ago, as a poor, frightened, troubled, runaway teen-ager."

Trixie nodded sadly. "I thought that exact same thing this afternoon, Honey, when I almost forgot about your father's generosity. It occurred to me then that loyalty must be a hard thing to ask of someone who's desperate for money."

"I keep remembering, too," Honey said, "that Regan ran away when Mr. Worthington appeared at the Manor House. That seems like the action of a guilty person."

"Not necessarily, Honey," Trixie replied. "Don't forget, Regan ran away to Saratoga. We know that much for sure. If he were running away for fear of being caught by Mr. Worthington, he could have gone to the Midwest or to California. There are racetracks and stables all over the country where he could find work. I still believe that his coming here shows that he's trying to clear himself."

"That's true," Honey agreed. "I guess I'd lost sight of that fact. Does that mean you're sure Regan is innocent?"

Trixie didn't answer for a long moment. "All I

can say," Trixie said finally, "is that I'm sure that the Regan we know couldn't drug a horse. The Regan of seven years ago might have been forced, by things he couldn't control, to do something that was against the law. But whatever the truth is, I want to know the whole story. And the only way to learn the whole story—"

"Is to find Regan," Honey concluded. "You're right, I know. It's—it's just so frightening to think that when we find Regan, he might confess to drugging Gadfly."

"We'll stand by Regan no matter what," Trixie said firmly. "But if we do find out that he was responsible, we'll have to convince him that he should turn himself in. I'm sure that your father will hire him the best lawyer in New York, and that a judge will take the circumstances—whatever they were—into account."

"But a judge will also take into account the fact that Regan ran away and stayed hidden for seven whole years. Besides, Trixie, I don't know if anyone could persuade Regan to do something he didn't want to do. What if he tells us that he is—or was— guilty of drugging Gadfly, and then refuses to turn himself in? What will we do then?"

As Trixie looked into Honey's searching eyes, her stomach tightened as she realized what their alternatives would be: either to turn Regan in against his will or have it on their consciences that they'd helped a guilty man escape.

"We'll cross that bridge when we come to it," Trixie said finally. Then she added silently, *And we may come to it tomorrow, if we find Regan.*

Complicated Theories · 12

THE NEXT MORNING at breakfast, following a plan they'd worked out the night before, Trixie and Honey told the Wheelers that they would prefer not to go to the track that day.

"We spent all day yesterday looking at those beautiful, beautiful horses on the track, and it was wonderful, but it made us miss riding," Honey explained in a wistful voice.

"So we'd like to find some place nearby where we can rent horses for a few hours and go riding," Trixie concluded, hoping that she had made her tone sound casual enough to keep the Wheelers from suspecting that she and Honey were keeping something secret from them.

"I don't understand," Mr. Wheeler said, frowning. "In just a few days, you'll be back at Sleepyside, with all the Manor House horses waiting for you, impatient to be exercised—especially now, with Regan gone. I don't know why you'd want to rent second-rate riding-academy horses and miss an entire afternoon of seeing the unique things that Saratoga has to offer."

Trixie felt her heart skip a beat, but she forced herself to keep her feelings of dismay from registering on her face. *Oh, please, Mr. Wheeler,* she thought, *don't tell us that we have to come to the track with you. Please, please!*

"Now, Matthew," Mrs. Wheeler said, putting her hand on her husband's arm, "this is the girls' vacation, and they should spend it as they like. Besides, I think that going out and getting some fresh air and exercise—even on what you call 'second-rate horses'—will be better for them than spending another day at a racetrack."

Mr. Wheeler looked from his wife's face to those of Honey and Trixie, which clearly reflected, in spite of their efforts to control their feelings, their eagerness to be on their own for the day. "I suppose you're right," he said finally. "When we've finished eating, you can ask the desk clerk for the names of some local riding stables."

Trixie hadn't realized that she'd been holding her

breath while she waited for Mr. Wheeler's decision. Now she let it out slowly while Honey said, "Thank you, Daddy! I can hardly wait! It's just a perfectly perfect day for riding."

"Thank you, Mr. Wheeler," Trixie echoed. "I hope you'll help us see the rest of the sights of Saratoga before we leave. It isn't that we aren't interested—really. It's just that all of yesterday's excitement has made us need to work off some steam."

Mr. Wheeler's face relaxed in a smile. "I guess I can understand, Trixie. It's just hard, sometimes, for grown-ups to remember the boundless energies of our youth. Have a good time."

The desk clerk gave the girls the names of four riding stables near town, and they quickly changed into their riding clothes, hailed a taxi, and gave the driver the address of the first place on their list. As they pulled away from the hotel, Trixie said, "I hope we get lucky before the fourth stable, or I'll wind up spending every cent I brought along for cab fare, instead of for souvenirs."

Honey nodded. "It could get expensive if we have to go to all four stables. But even if we do spend all our money, can you think of anything that the people in Sleepyside would rather have us bring back than Regan?"

Trixie squeezed her friend's hand. "That's a

wonderful thought, Honey. And it's stupid of me to be worried about money at a time like this, when we're right on the verge of finding Regan."

Nevertheless, when Trixie checked the dwindling contents of her billfold an hour and a half later, she admitted to herself both that she was worried about running out of money and that they seemed no closer to finding Regan than ever.

The girls had visited the first two stables on their list, once again relying on the plan they'd formulated the night before. They knew that they couldn't just walk into the stables and ask for Regan by name, since he was almost sure to be working under an alias. So they had decided they would simply say that they wanted to rent horses and would ask to look over the stock to select the ones they wanted. That would give them time to look around and ask subtle questions about the employees. It was risky, they knew, because they could miss Regan if it was his day off or if he was running errands away from the stables, and because they risked arousing the curiosity of his employers with a badly worded question. But they had decided it was all they could do.

Now, in the taxi on the way to the third place on their list, Trixie had to wonder if their plan had been as well thought-out as it had seemed. They had caught no glimpse of the redheaded groom, and their questions regarding the size of the staff at each of the two stables had brought no information that they could use.

"The worst part, Honey," Trixie complained after they had given the driver the third address, "is that we don't even know for sure that we can eliminate these first two places. I mean, Regan could be working at either one of them. The fact that we didn't find him doesn't prove anything."

"I know, Trixie," Honey said. "But we still have two chances out of four to find him. And if we don't find him today—well, as you said to me last night, we'll cross that bridge when we come to it."

The cab pulled into the long driveway of the third riding stable and stopped in front of the office. The girls once again dug into their billfolds to pay the driver, both noting sadly the few bills remaining. They climbed out and looked around for someone to ask their by now well-rehearsed questions. Trixie heard a small squeal from Honey, and she followed her friend's gaze to a large fenced exercise yard to their left. There, cantering around in a wide circle on an Appaloosa horse, was Regan!

Honey lunged forward to run to the fence, but Trixie grabbed her arm and stopped her. She whispered into Honey's ear, and Honey's face dissolved into a wide grin, her hazel eyes twinkling.

The two girls walked quietly, almost on tiptoe, to the fence and arranged themselves in casual watching postures, their feet on the bottom rail of the fence and their elbows resting on the top.

So intent was Regan on his riding that he made two more broad passes around the yard before he noticed the girls. On the third pass, he glanced over at them. Then the girls saw Regan do something they had never seen him do before and wouldn't have believed he possibly could do: Looking back over his shoulder to confirm what his first glance had told him, Regan lost his balance and fell off the horse!

He scrambled quickly to his feet and caught the horse's reins. The expression on his face changed from astonishment to embarrassment to anger. Then he threw back his head and laughed, and the girls scrambled over the fence and ran to embrace him.

"You girls are a sight for sore eyes!" he exclaimed. "Although my eyes won't be the only part of me that's sore tomorrow, after that spill I just took. How in the world did you happen to come to this place?"

"By taxi," Trixie said teasingly.

"After we went to two other riding stables looking for you," Honey added.

"*After* a certain chatty cabdriver at the track told us about a nice young redheaded man who perfumed his cab with horse scent he brought with him from the boarding stable where he worked," Trixie concluded.

Regan looked from one girl to the other as their jumbled explanation flew back and forth. Then he shook his head. "You'd better come back to the stable with me and explain the whole thing—slowly—while I curry this horse."

While Regan worked, the girls told him how they'd traced him to this spot, starting with their walk through Saratoga and their finding his boots in the pawnshop.

"We were afraid something might have happened to you, Regan, because the pawnbroker's description of the man who brought the boots in didn't fit you at all," Trixie said.

"It wasn't me," Regan said. "It was Johnny, who's an exercise boy here at the stable. He and I have gotten to be pretty good friends since I started working here. Johnny's not much of a talker, and I don't think he managed to get much schoolroom education, so most people treat him as though he's plain stupid. But I spotted him as a good man with horses. I respect him for that, and I let him know it. He was grateful for the encouragement, and he's done everything he could to help me out. I was a little short of cash when I first got here. Johnny offered to loan me some money, but he doesn't have much himself. So I asked him if he'd take the boots in for me and bring me back the money, which he did, no questions asked. My old boots are plenty good enough for the work I do around here. But I plan to get my good boots back as soon as I get my first paycheck.

"But wait a minute," Regan said suddenly. "You girls have done a first-rate detective job in tracing me here, with nothing to go on but a pair of monogrammed boots in a pawnshop window. But that doesn't explain how you came to be in Saratoga in the first place."

In their joy at finally finding Regan, and their pride in relating the detecting process that had led them to him, the girls had forgotten the shadow of accusation that still hung over their friend's head. The smiles left their faces, and they stared at the ground, neither one wanting to introduce the unpleasant topic.

"Come on, girls. Out with it!" Regan demanded. "Is this a pleasure jaunt, or did you manage to trail me from Sleepyside to Saratoga, too?"

Trixie took a deep breath, then blurted out the rest of the story: their hunch that Mr. Worthington was connected with Regan's disappearance; the information in the book at the Sleepyside library; the invitation they'd wangled to join the Wheelers in Saratoga; and, finally, Carl Stinson's accusations against Regan the day before.

As he listened, Regan's face turned almost the same fiery red as his hair. When Trixie had finished, the only sound for a few moments was that of the currycomb against the Appaloosa's coat as

Regan waited for his rage to subside enough so that he could speak. Finally, he threw the currycomb into the equipment box and stalked out of the stable, beckoning the girls to follow him.

He led them into the office, where he poured himself a cup of coffee from a large urn and gave each of the girls a soft drink from a well-stocked refrigerator. Then he sat down at a battered wooden table, and the girls took chairs on the opposite side.

"You girls have done a remarkable job of piecing this story together," Regan began, "but there are a few things you don't know. For one thing, the race that Gadfly ran when he was doped seven years ago was a claiming race. Do you know what that is?"

Honey nodded, but Trixie shook her head.

"It's a pretty common type of race, Trixie," Regan said, "because the care and upkeep of a Thoroughbred racehorse is so expensive, and so many things can damage a horse, that owners have to weed out their stables constantly to keep from falling into debt.

"Here's how it works: The track announces that there will be, say, a five-thousand-dollar claiming race. That means that the winner of the race can be purchased for five thousand dollars by anyone who submits a sealed bid to the track officials before the race. Any owner who enters the race knows that if his horse wins, someone might claim him.

"So it becomes a game of chance—and trickery. Sometimes an owner will enter an unsound horse in hopes that it will win and be claimed by someone who thinks it's worth more than it is. And sometimes an owner will enter a sound horse, one that's far superior to the other horses in the field, in hopes that it can win against the lesser horses and yet not be claimed, because people will think there's something wrong with it."

"Whew!" Trixie exclaimed. "This is as confusing as watching the workouts at the track yesterday morning. I don't see how the owners can fool each other, though. I mean, they all know about horses. Surely they can tell whether one is sound or not."

Regan shook his head. "You don't know the lengths that owners will go to, Trix. An owner who wants his good horse to win without being claimed might bandage one of its legs for days before the race, to make it look as though it's injured. And an owner who wants an unsound horse claimed will use ice packs, medication, even ultraviolet rays to treat a bad shoulder or a sore knee so that the horse will look good for a few days before the race. And don't forget, anyone who puts in a bid for a horse is risking paying a lot of money for something that may or may not pay back the investment. I used a five-thousand-dollar claiming race as an example, but it might be as high as twenty-five thousand, which is what Gadfly was entered for."

"Whew!" Trixie exclaimed again.

"But what does the fact that it was a claiming race have to do with Gadfly's being drugged, Regan?" Honey asked.

"I don't know for sure, Honey," Regan answered. "But the rumors that were going around right before the race put a few other people besides me in a suspicious light.

"For one thing, there was a rumor that Mr. Worthington was having some financial problems right around the time of that race. He speculates on the stock market, you know, and I heard he'd dropped a bundle. Also, Gadfly had been having a knee problem. Carl Stinson thought it would clear up, but Worthington disagreed. I heard them arguing about it one afternoon a couple of weeks before the race—shortly before Gadfly was entered."

"I'm not following you very well," Trixie confessed. "Did the rumors and the argument you overheard make you suspicious of Mr. Worthington or Mr. Stinson?"

"Both," Regan replied. "The facts against Stinson are that he'd never really had a great horse to work with before, and he believed very much in Gadfly. So he could have drugged the horse, knowing that the finding of the drugs in the horse's system would disqualify any claim. He wouldn't have figured, of course, that the six-month suspension would completely ruin the horse's spirit and bring his racing career to an early end.

"My reasons for suspecting Worthington are a little more complicated, because he's a more complex man. One thing that's occurred to me is that his finances could have taken a turn for the better right before the race, so he'd have been able to take the risk of keeping Gadfly for a while to see if the knee did respond to treatment."

"But then couldn't he have just withdrawn the horse from the race?" Honey asked.

"He could have," Regan said. "But you have to remember that Mr. Worthington is a very rich and powerful man. He's used to giving orders, not taking them. And he knows that Carl Stinson is the backbone of Worthington Farms. If he did decide that he didn't want Gadfly claimed, he could have drugged the horse to break the trainer's spirit."

"Huh?" Trixie asked, totally confused.

"According to racing regulations, the trainer of a horse that is drugged is automatically considered responsible, and he's suspended from the track pending an investigation. By drugging Gadfly, Worthington would get revenge on Stinson for arguing with him, and at the same time he'd make it financially impossible for Carl to leave, since the six-month suspension from racing would also mean a six-month loss in his commissions from the horses' earnings."

"Whew!" Trixie exclaimed for the third time.

Regan chuckled wryly. "I told you the reasons for my suspicions are complicated. I think you can see why I wasn't too eager to hang around and try to explain my theories to the racing commission. It would have been the jumbled theories of a seventeen-year-old groom against the reputations of a wealthy horse owner and an established, respected trainer.

"It was natural for them to suspect me, in a way. I was young, I came to work for Worthington and Stinson out of nowhere, and I was the only person aside from them who had access to Gadfly right before the race. I knew I was innocent, but I also knew it would be hard to prove. And the only two people in the world who could have an interest in defending me against the charges were the same two people that I myself suspected of the crime." Regan was silent for a moment. He swirled the last of his coffee in the bottom of the cup, staring at the circling liquid. He set the cup down on the table with a bang, then concluded, "So I ran."

"But you came back," Trixie said softly.

Regan nodded. "When I heard that Worthington was coming to the Manor House, the whole thing came flooding back over me—all the fear and confusion I'd felt seven years ago. But then I stopped and thought about it, and I realized that I'm not a scared, confused kid anymore. I'm a man, with friends and responsibilities. For their sake, and for mine, I knew I couldn't live with the suspicions anymore. So I came back to clear my name."

"Have you found any evidence yet to help you do that?" Trixie asked eagerly.

"No," Regan said shortly. "This red head of mine makes me pretty recognizable. I haven't been able to do as much snooping as I'd like because I'm afraid someone I knew seven years ago might spot me and turn me in. Then I'd be right back where I started.

"About the only thing of interest I've turned up might turn out to be a coincidence. Seven years ago, there was a tough-looking fellow hanging around the Worthington stables. I never knew his name or figured out what his connection with Worthington was, if there was one. But I got the feeling that he was up to no good. And yesterday when I went to the track, I spotted him again."

"Are you sure it was the same man?" Honey asked. "Seven years is a long time, after all."

"There's no mistaking this guy," Regan told her. "He has a long, ugly scar running down the side of his face."

"I saw him!" Trixie exclaimed. "I saw him yesterday at the track, too. Remember, Honey? The same cabdriver who told us about giving a ride to Regan told us he'd driven that guy to the track. I bet if we found that taxi driver again, he'd be able to tell us—"

"Hold it right there," Regan interrupted. "Trixie, I appreciate everything you've gone through to find me, and I appreciate your trying to believe I was innocent, when a lot of people said I wasn't. I'm glad you found me. Seeing you girls has done me a world of good. It's reminded me of how much I want to clear myself so that I can go home, to Sleepyside and the Manor House."

"But?" Trixie queried.

"But," Regan said firmly, "I don't want you to get involved with that man. Racetrack hoodlums are as tough as they come. I'd never forgive myself if something happened to you girls while you were trying to help me out. Don't try to find that man, Trixie. Promise me you won't."

"I—I promise," Trixie said reluctantly.

"Good girl," Regan said. "I'll clear myself in due time, and I'll be back at the Manor House as soon as I do. And I want both of you to promise me something else. Promise me you won't tell anyone where I am. The only way I can hope to clear myself is to stay undercover a while longer."

"We won't tell anyone," Trixie said quickly.

"I wanted to tell my parents we'd found your boots, but Trixie stopped me," Honey confessed. "I'm glad she did."

"Me, too," Regan said. "But for heaven's sake, don't feel bad because you wanted to confide in your parents, Honey. It was the right thing to do.

We'll tell them everything soon, believe me. And now," he concluded, rising from the table, "I'd better call you girls a cab so you can get back to town."

An Old Romance · 13

RELUCTANTLY, Honey and Trixie got into the backseat of the taxi, after giving Regan one last hug. As the cab pulled away, they knelt on the backseat and waved to their friend until the cab turned a corner and he was lost from their sight.

Turning and sitting down on the backseat, Trixie sighed happily. "Well, Honey, the first part of our mission is accomplished. We found—" Trixie glanced at the cabdriver— "we found our friend and got his side of the story."

Honey nodded. "It's amazing, Trixie. As soon as I saw him, all my doubts and suspicions just vanished, and I knew he was innocent. Our first hunch, back in Sleepyside, was the right one after all: He ran just because he was young and scared, not because he had a gambling problem or resented his boss or any of the other theories we came up with later."

"I think that's an important lesson for us, Honey," Trixie said. "What your heart tells you about someone is usually right. Later on, when your head gets into the act, you start thinking up all kinds of wild theories that are logical enough but just not true."

"We should try to remember that," Honey said. "But we shouldn't discount all the 'wild theories' we've had since we came to Saratoga. Following up on them helped us solve our mystery."

"Part one of our mystery," Trixie corrected her. "We know now that our friend didn't do what he's been accused of doing, but we still have to find out who did."

"Trixie, you promised!" Honey wailed. "Not five minutes ago you said you wouldn't get involved!"

"I said I wouldn't get involved with the scar-faced man," Trixie pointed out, "and that's a promise I'm only too happy to keep." She shuddered. "I don't need to be told that he's out of my league. But don't forget, there are a couple of other suspects in this case that we're in a perfect position to keep an eye on, and I intend to do just that."

Honey shook her head in mock exasperation, but

there was a smile on her face as she said, "Trixie Belden, if the criminals we chase were half as sneaky as you are, they'd all commit perfect crimes and never get caught."

"Why, what do you mean?" Trixie asked, her blue eyes rounded innocently.

"You know what I mean," Honey said sternly. "Every time someone makes you promise to stay out of trouble, it turns out you've found a loophole that will let you go charging right ahead without breaking the promise." Honey sighed. "I don't suppose you have any tricky ideas for breaking our promise not to tell my parents what we know, if we think we should."

Trixie shook her head. "That's one promise we have to keep, Honey. Remember what Dan said to us outside the library back in Sleepyside? If someone's grown up poor and afraid, they've also built up a lack of faith in people that's hard to overcome. You and I tend to trust people, because our experience tells us that most people are good and kind and will believe us when we tell them the truth. Regan's only had that experience since he took the job with your parents. He still has a lot of mistrust to overcome. If your parents try to contact him—or worse yet, if they decide to bring the police or the racing association in on the case—Regan will run again. I'm sure of it."

"I know all that," Honey said. "But I know, too,

that Regan's chances of clearing himself aren't helped by his own fear of being recognized. And our chances of clearing him are pretty dim; we're fourteen-year-old girls who'll be going up against some very tough customers."

Trixie leaned her head against the back of the seat and closed her eyes. "People always think detective work is just a matter of finding out what the truth is," she said mournfully. "But in this case, we have more truths than we need. The problem is trying to figure out how to deal with them." She lifted her head and looked at Honey resolutely. "I'll tell you what," she said. "We'll keep working on the case until this so-called vacation is over and it's time for us to go back to Sleepyside. If nothing has fallen into place by then, we'll have another discussion about telling your parents. How's that?"

"I guess it'll have to do," Honey said reluctantly as the taxi pulled up in front of their hotel. "But from now on, I'm going to keep my fingers crossed whenever I make a promise."

At the hotel desk, the girls found another note from the Wheelers. Honey waited until they were in their room before she unfolded it and scanned it quickly. "Oh, no," she moaned.

"What is it?" Trixie asked. "Is something wrong?"

"Not exactly," Honey replied. "At least, I'm sure Daddy didn't think so when he wrote this note. He's arranged another surprise for us: We're to have dinner tonight with Mr. Worthington, Mr. Stinson, and Mr. Stinson's daughter, Joan."

"Oh, woe." Trixie looked stricken. "Honey, I can't stand it. Let's think of some excuse for not going—let's say we're both sick or something. I simply can't sit around a dinner table, tonight of all nights, and make small talk with the two men Regan suspects of trying to frame him."

"We have to, Trixie," Honey said. "For one thing, it's our duty as detectives. We have to be there to listen to what Worthington and Stinson say, in case they drop any information. And we also have to be there to *keep* them from dropping one specific piece of information."

"Gleeps!" Trixie cried, following Honey's thoughts. "Regan's name! Why didn't I think of that before? If Stinson mentions Regan in front of your parents, like he did in front of us yesterday, the whole story will come out. If your parents find out Regan used to work for Worthington Farms, they're sure to realize that Regan left the Manor House the same day Mr. Worthington came to visit, and they'll probably decide that he ran because he was guilty. Regan might lose his job. They might even call in the police. Oh, woe!" She slumped despondently on the bed.

Honey nodded, her face solemn. "I wasn't worried before, because I know that Daddy feels very

strongly about respecting other people's privacy.
He wouldn't volunteer the story of Regan's disappearance to someone he doesn't know very well,
like Mr. Worthington, because he'd feel that it
wasn't his story to tell. Carl Stinson obviously
doesn't feel that way, since he told us all about
Regan the first time we ever met him. So we have to
be there tonight, Trixie."

"We might as well start getting ready," Trixie
said. "At least tonight, I'm too worried about
everything else to care how I look."

By the time the dessert was served at the restaurant that evening, the girls realized that they
could easily have left the Wheelers alone with Carl
Stinson without worrying about what he might say.
The trainer was in a silent, sullen mood. Aside from
answering a few questions with a yes or a no and
giving the waiter his order, Stinson had not spoken
all evening. His daughter, a pretty, intelligent
young woman, had tried to fill in the awkward
gaps in the conversation, but she had grown in-
creasingly embarrassed at her father's behavior,
and finally she, too, was silent.

Trixie and Honey said very little, afraid that they
might accidentally bring up a topic of conversation
that would lead the trainer to another outburst
against Regan. Thus, it was Mr. and Mrs. Wheeler
and Mr. Worthington who did most of the talking,

with Worthington dominating the discussion.

On the surface, the man seemed as friendly and charming as he had the day before at the track. But with Regan's description of him echoing in her mind, Trixie found herself looking at him—and listening to him—in a different way. He was, indeed, a man who liked to give orders rather than take them. He had chosen the restaurant, and he and the Stinsons had been waiting when the others arrived. Worthington took charge immediately, instructing everyone on where to sit and what to order from the menu.

Maybe he's just trying to make us all feel comfortable, Trixie thought. But if that was Worthington's intention, he was failing—in Trixie's opinion, at least. She felt suffocated, as though her entire evening were being planned to the last detail without regard to what she herself wanted.

Trixie found herself remembering the incident at lunch the day before, when she'd asked Worthington if he'd rather have losing seasons at the track than risk losing his trainer. The angry look that had crossed his face had frightened her then, and she found herself giving in to his orders at the restaurant to keep from seeing it again.

A large ego and a bad temper, Trixie thought. *A combination like that makes for a person who could seek revenge.*

"That was a lovely meal," Joan Stinson said,

bringing Trixie's thoughts back to the table. "But I overate, as usual, and I'd like to take a walk to help my digestion. Would you girls care to join me?"

Eager to get away from the silent trainer and his overbearing employer, the girls readily agreed.

The restaurant was built around a small court-yard with carefully tended flowers and shrubs and a small, man-made stream. It was there that Joan, Honey, and Trixie walked, silent at first, until Joan Stinson broke the stillness of the summer evening.

"I feel that I should apologize for my father's behavior during dinner. He made me feel terribly uncomfortable, and I assume that everyone else was feeling the same way. He has a lot on his mind tonight. Mr. Worthington just told him that he's entered my father's favorite horse in a claiming race the day after tomorrow."

"Not Gadbox!" Honey exclaimed.

"What do you mean—*just* told him?" Trixie asked at the same time.

Joan smiled wryly. "Yes, Gadbox, and just this evening, to answer both your questions. Mr. Worthington offered us a ride to the restaurant, then broke the news to us on the way. I wouldn't put it past him if he planned the whole thing that way," she added, her voice suddenly bitter, "telling us on the way here so that my father couldn't voice his objections."

"But why would Mr. Worthington enter Gadbox

in a claiming race?" Trixie asked. "We just saw him race yesterday, and he was fantastic. He won easily!"

Joan Stinson shrugged. "J. T. Worthington is not a man who feels he must explain himself to his hired help," she said. "He pulled this same trick seven years ago, right after my mother died. It cost my father his self-respect and a chance to become an owner instead of just a trainer, and I always believed it cost me, at least indirectly, the man I was in love with."

Honey and Trixie exchanged stunned glances. Could Joan Stinson be talking about Regan?

"The man you loved?" Honey prompted softly.

Joan Stinson laughed mirthlessly. "Forgive me. I'm being overly dramatic, I suppose. Regan wasn't really a man at the time. He was a seventeen-year-old boy. And I was only sixteen, so what I think of as true love may have been just a childish infatuation. But I never got the chance to find out. Against my father's wishes, Mr. Worthington entered a horse in a claiming race. After the race, it was discovered that the horse had been drugged. Suspicion turned to Regan, and he ran away, without even telling me good-bye. I didn't believe that he was guilty. I still don't. But I never got a chance to tell him that, either."

Trixie felt suddenly dizzy as she tried to accept this stunning revelation about Regan's past.

This beautiful young woman had once been in love with Regan. Trixie had often wondered why Regan never dated any of the eligible women in Sleepyside. She was sure that any of them would be happy to accept an invitation from the handsome groom. *Maybe this is the answer*, Trixie thought. *Maybe Regan has never forgotten Joan, just as she's never forgotten him.* When the mystery was solved, Trixie vowed silently, she'd see to it that Regan and Joan had a chance to meet once again.

Trixie caught Honey's eye, and she could tell from her friend's expression that Honey had just made a similar vow.

"Don't you have any idea why Mr. Worthington made the decision to enter Gadbox in the claiming race?" Honey prompted.

The muscles in Joan Stinson's jaw tightened. "Oh, I have an idea, all right," she said harshly. "I think Mr. Worthington is afraid of letting my father have a winning horse, because he's afraid that Daddy will use the winnings to get out from under the great man's thumb. I think he'll wait just a few more years, until Daddy is too old to think about leaving Worthington Farms to establish a stable of his own. Then he'll start letting my father keep his winning horses. But then it'll be too late. My father will be an old and broken man whose dreams have passed him by, and J. T. Worthington will line his own pockets with the winnings that my father should have earned for himself."

"That's enough, Joan!" Carl Stinson barked.

Honey, Trixie, and Joan whirled around to see the trainer standing in the entrance to the court-yard, his face reflecting his struggle to control his anger. "We're going home."

"All right," Joan said, making an effort to keep her voice calm. "Just let me go back inside and say good-bye to—"

"You've said enough already," her father said sharply. "Let's go."

Joan walked quickly to the doorway, her head lowered in embarrassment.

Carl Stinson turned and gave the girls a long, harsh glare, then followed his daughter out of the restaurant.

The two girls stood in shocked silence for a long moment after the Stinsons had disappeared.

"You can't say we haven't learned a lot tonight," Honey said finally.

"And I don't much like what we've learned," Trixie added. "There're an awful lot of bad feelings between Mr. Worthington and Mr. Stinson, from what Joan said. Who knows what either of them might have done seven years ago for revenge?"

"That's not all, Trixie," Honey added, her eyes cloudy with fear. "Who knows what they might do before the claiming race this week?"

Trixie felt a wave of terror go through her as the

meaning of Honey's words struck her. This new claiming race could end in the same kind of tragedy as the other one had, seven years ago. *Or something even worse*, Trixie thought. *At least seven years ago no lives were lost.* She shuddered.

"All we can do is keep our eyes open," Honey said helplessly.

"Wide open," Trixie added.

Captured! • 14

THE NEXT MORNING, Trixie and Honey responded eagerly to Mr. Wheeler's invitation to accompany him to the track. "It's good to see that you've got your need for exercise out of your systems," Mr. Wheeler teased.

Trixie felt herself turning red as she remembered guiltily that she and Honey had never actually got around to riding the day before. *Does Mr. Wheeler suspect anything?* she thought. Looking at him intently, she decided not. *Just because I've begun to suspect everybody of everything since I got involved with this mystery, I think everyone else is suspicious, too. That's just plain silly.*

Trixie's own suspicions were not lessened by what she found at the track, however. As the girls and Mr. Wheeler approached the stables where the Worthington Farms horses were kept, they discovered Mr. Worthington and his trainer in the midst of a heated argument.

As soon as Mr. Worthington saw them, he broke off his argument in mid-sentence and forced his face into a slick, charming smile. Carl Stinson, still scowling, turned and stalked away.

"Good morning, good morning," Worthington said with exaggerated cheerfulness. "My trainer and I were just having a little, shall we say, difference of opinion. After twenty years, Carl sometimes forgets who's boss."

And you sometimes forget how much you owe him, Trixie thought angrily.

Mr. Worthington noticed Trixie's scowling look, and he looked flustered for a moment. He soon recovered his composure, however, and was as outgoing as ever as he escorted them to the workouts, bought them lunch, and then settled down with them in his private box to watch the races.

Honey, always tactful, managed to enter into the stream of small talk that Mr. Worthington and Mr. Wheeler exchanged. Trixie knew that she was being ungracious and risking hurting Mr. Wheeler's feelings with her silence, but her resentment of Worthington's attitude, coupled with her resolve to keep her eyes open for clues, made it almost impossible for her to think of anything to say. She pretended to concentrate on the races, cheering when the crowd cheered, but her mind was busy working over the mystery. She constantly scanned the crowd for a glimpse of the scar-faced man.

She had no luck in finding him, however, until after the last race, when she and the Wheelers accompanied Mr. Worthington back to the Worthington Farms stalls. Suddenly, out of the corner of her eye, she spotted the scar-faced man lurking near Gadbox's stall. She nudged Honey, her mind searching frantically for an excuse to leave Mr. Worthington's side in pursuit of the man.

Her mind went blank, and even Honey's usual diplomacy failed her. The two girls stood in desperate silence as the man disappeared into the crowd.

For the next several hours, the girls faced the same frustrating situation they'd found themselves in the first time they'd gone to the track: Unable to find any time alone, they couldn't discuss the scar-faced man's appearance and disappearance.

It was not until after dinner, when the girls were alone in their room, that they were able to talk. Then, it was hard for them to know what to say. They both agreed that the bad feeling between Worthington and his trainer was building to the breaking point. They agreed, too, that the appearance of the scar-faced man near Gadbox's stall the day before the claiming race was certainly a cause for suspicion. But what could they do about their worries?

"The claiming race is tomorrow, Honey," Trixie pointed out. "That means, if something is going to happen, it will happen tonight. And it will happen at the track, which is exactly where I think we should be."

"Oh, Trixie, I don't know," Honey responded. "That sounds awfully dangerous to me. Besides, if we go to the track because we think the scar-faced man might be there, we'll be breaking our promise to Regan."

"No, we won't," Trixie said. "I told you, Honey, I have no desire to get involved with that man. If we do see him, we'll go get the police. We might not see him, anyway. For my money, the culprit in this case is just as likely to be Carl Stinson or even J. T. Worthington himself."

Honey sighed, unable to refute her friend's usual evasive logic. "Okay, Trixie," she said. "Let's say we won't be in the slightest bit of danger and we won't even be bending our promise to Regan, let alone breaking it—although I don't know if I really believe either of those statements. How do you suggest we get out of this hotel, past the front desk, and out to the track without being stopped and returned to my parents, who would lock us in our hotel room or return us to Sleepyside in handcuffs to keep us out of further mischief?"

In spite of her tension, Trixie giggled. "They might even ask Sergeant Molinson to lock us up in jail for disturbing the peace. Knowing Sergeant Molinson, I think he'd probably do it, too!"

Honey's mouth curved upward in a smile, but she forced herself to sound stern. "Don't change the subject, Trixie. How will we get to the track without being seen?"

"I have that all figured out," Trixie replied eagerly. "We'll wait a couple of hours, until your parents think we're asleep. Then we'll go down the back stairs, which come out in back of the hotel." Trixie grinned sheepishly. "I checked that out when you were showering before dinner. We'll walk a block or two from the hotel, so no one will know where we came from, and then we'll catch a taxi to the track."

"And what if the cabdriver asks us why we want to go to the track hours after it's closed?"

Trixie shrugged. "We'll tell him we're going there to meet someone. That's true, in a way."

"You win, Trixie," Honey said, "if only because it would be a shame to let all that careful planning go to waste."

Two hours later, Honey and Trixie, both dressed in blue jeans, sneakers, and T-shirts, walked quickly down the back stairs of the hotel and out onto the street. Even in the middle of town, the stillness of the August night seemed mysterious and frightening. Trixie took a deep breath to calm her suddenly jittery stomach. A block from the hotel, she flagged down a cab. She and Honey climbed into the backseat, and Trixie said, "To the racetrack, please."

The two girls waited fearfully for the driver to ask the reason for their strange destination, but he simply turned down the flag on the meter and moved off into the dark night. *That's one hurdle out of the way*, Trixie thought. *How many do we have left to go?*

At the track, the girls paid the driver, then looked around for a way to enter the track. They had to walk completely around the fenced-in enclosure before they found a place where they could scale the fence.

Once inside the track area, the girls stood still for a moment, unsure which way to go to find Gadbox's stall. Finally, Honey tapped Trixie's shoulder and pointed to the left, her eyebrows raised as a signal that she was still not entirely sure of her directions. Trixie shrugged and nodded her agreement that that was as good a place to start as any, and the two moved silently across the deserted enclosure.

The girls had gone some distance before their surroundings began to look familiar. Trixie tapped Honey's arm and pointed to the right. The Worthington stalls were right around the corner of the barn they were walking past—she thought.

Rounding the corner, Trixie spotted the Worthington stalls, exactly where she'd thought they'd be. *Home free*, she thought—just as a shadowy figure stepped out of the darkness, clapped a hand across each girl's mouth, and dragged them, stumbling, into an empty stall.

Trixie and Honey both fell backward into a mound of fresh, clean straw. Looking up, Trixie saw a man's form towering above her, hands on hips. The moonlight that streamed in through the open doorway outlined his figure and glinted on his bright red hair.

Regan! Trixie thought, her heart pounding so hard that she thought her ribs would be shattered by the pressure. *Oh, no, Regan! We were so sure you were innocent!*

Regan knelt in the straw in front of the girls, his face a stony mask. Trixie felt herself cringing away from him. At the sight of her terror, Regan's expression changed to one of sympathy. "Hey, Trix," he whispered, "don't be frightened. I'm sorry I grabbed you out there. I didn't recognize you in the dark. I guess I don't have to ask what you two are doing here. You heard about the claiming race and came out to try to catch someone drugging Gadbox, right?"

Wordlessly, Trixie and Honey nodded.

"Me, too," Regan said. Then he sighed. "I thought I'd caught my culprits, too—and who do I find but the girl detectives from Sleepyside!"

Of course! Trixie thought, tears of relief welling in her eyes. *Regan isn't here to drug Gadbox; he's here to catch someone else doing it, just as Honey and I are!*

"Oh, Regan, I'm so glad!" Honey whispered in the darkness.

"Well, I'm not," Regan said. "This isn't a safe place for you girls to be tonight. I'd send you home, but I'm afraid you'd come right back, anyhow. So you two might as well stay—but keep close to me, do you hear?"

Again the girls nodded, scrambling to their feet.

Putting a finger to his lips to remind them of the need for silence, Regan turned and left the stall. Trixie and Honey followed close behind him, their own breathing sounding thunderous in their ears.

As they neared the stall where Gadbox was kept, the three heard voices. Exchanging startled looks, they flattened themselves against the wall of an adjoining barn and held their breaths as they listened.

"I give up," a gruff-voiced man was saying. "We've searched every inch of this stall, and we haven't found the feed pouch. Since that other race, Stinson probably sleeps with the feed bag under his pillow the night before a big race." The gruff-voiced man laughed stupidly.

"Keep your voice down!" a second man hissed. "And keep looking! We stand to make a bundle on tomorrow's race. All we have to do is find that feed pouch. It's too bad there isn't some dumb kid around to take the rap for us this time."

Trixie felt Regan's body go rigid with anger. She reached out a hand to him, but she was too late. Regan had charged forward. "You'll take the rap for this one yourselves!" he shouted.

Watching from the shadows, Trixie saw a man emerge from Gadbox's stall, a gun in his hand. *Scarface!* Trixie thought. She closed her eyes, not wanting to see the flash of fire from the gun's muzzle. Instead, she heard a dull thud as the scar-faced man hit Regan over the head with the gun.

We have to get out of here, Trixie thought, panic-stricken. *We have to get help.* "Run, Honey," she whispered hoarsely.

The girls began to run, but they hadn't gone more than ten yards before the scar-faced man overtook them, forcing them roughly to the ground with a flying tackle.

Stranded · 15

TRIXIE AND HONEY struggled with all their might to break loose from their captor's grasp. "Louie!" the man shouted. "Get out here on the double! And bring some rope!"

Still struggling, Trixie heard the sound of running feet approaching, and then she was yanked to her feet by the second man, while the man who had tackled them hauled Honey to a standing position. The first man, Trixie saw in the darkness, was Scarface. She twisted her head to look over her shoulder at Louie, his accomplice, who was tying her hands behind her back. He was a small man, but the strength with which he grasped her arms told her that his size was deceptive.

Trixie's teeth were chattering with fear, but she clenched her jaw to keep them quiet. *We can't let them know that we're afraid*, she thought. *We can't even let ourselves be afraid. We have to keep our heads clear and keep looking for a way out of this.*

The small man had finished tying Trixie's hands; he cut off the leftover rope with a pocketknife and tossed it to the scar-faced man, who tied Honey.

"What do we do now, boss?" Louie asked.

"There's an empty horse trailer behind the barn, still hitched to a pickup truck. We'll put our nosy friends in that until we find the feed bag and put the dope in it. Then we'll all go for a little ride. But only two of us'll come back." Laughing at his own attempt at humor, Scarface pulled Honey along with him to the trailer, and Louie followed with Trixie in tow.

The girls were thrown roughly into the trailer, and they lay silent for a moment. Then they heard footsteps approaching again, and they moved out of the way as Regan's unconscious body landed in a crumpled heap in the trailer.

"I-Is he still alive, Trixie?" Honey whispered, her voice trembling.

Trixie wormed her way over to where Regan lay and maneuvered her bound hands to the pulse on his neck, which was throbbing steadily. "He's all right!" she whispered joyfully. "But I don't think it's a good sign that he's been unconscious this long."

As if in reply, Regan moaned and pulled himself slowly to a sitting position, his hands held to his head. "Wh-What happened?" he groaned. "Where am I?"

"You're all right," Trixie repeated. "The man with the scar hit you over the head with his gun. He and his accomplice put us in a horse trailer, and as soon as they put the drugs in Gadbox's feed bag, they're going to—to take us somewhere," she finished lamely, not wanting to repeat the threatening words that Scarface had spoken.

"Regan," Honey whispered urgently, "Trixie and I are tied up. Can you untie us? We have to try to get out of here before those men come back."

Trixie turned her back to Regan and held out her hands. The young groom fumbled with the knots, but still weakened and confused from the blow to his head, he was unable even to loosen the ropes.

"Did I make those knots too tight for you?" Louie's voice, followed by his stupid laugh, broke Regan's and the girls' rapt concentration. "Well, I brought some more rope, to tie some more knots with. We'll see what kind of luck you have with those."

Louie forced Regan to lie on his stomach. He tied Regan's hands behind him, then bent his legs up behind him and tied his feet to his hands. "Just like the calf-roping at the rodeo," Louie chuckled. Louie bound the girls' feet with two more lengths of rope and was proudly surveying his handiwork, when the man with the scar poked his head into the trailer.

"All finished?" Scarface asked.

Louie nodded. "It'll hold 'em for a while—a good long while, I'd say."

"Good," Scarface said curtly. "The drug is mixed in with the feed. If everything works the way we figured, Gadbox will have just enough dope in his system to show up in the urine test after the race. Then he'll be disqualified."

"What are you going to do with us?" Trixie demanded nervously.

"There's a deserted barn out in the country. We'll dump you there. By the time anybody finds you, the two of us will be headed out of the country, where we'll live like kings until the heat blows over. Any other questions?" Scarface asked sarcastically. Without waiting for a reply, Scarface signaled to Louie, and the two men disappeared.

Her face burning, Trixie forced herself to remain silent, but her mind was working frantically. She and Regan and Honey were in no immediate danger, but Gadbox would be disqualified. "And possibly ruined as a racehorse, just as his father was," she murmured.

"Gadbox isn't the only one who'll be ruined,"

Regan's voice said, startling Trixie, who hadn't realized she'd spoken out loud.

"What do you mean, Regan?" Honey asked.

Just then the engine of the pickup truck turned over, and the trailer lurched as it moved forward. The two girls were knocked off balance by the movement, and they struggled to right themselves.

"Who else will be ruined?" Trixie demanded as soon as she recovered.

"If Gadbox is disqualified tomorrow, it will be the second time in seven years that a Worthington Farms horse has been drugged during a claiming race. The first case went unsolved, but the track officials will be too embarrassed to let that happen a second time. They'll look hard for someone to pin the crime on—maybe Worthington, maybe Stinson." Regan laughed hollowly. "Maybe even me, if the investigation turns up the fact that I was back in Saratoga."

"But Regan, the track officials wouldn't accuse someone who wasn't guilty of the crime," Trixie protested.

"Of course not," Regan said. "They won't prosecute unless they have sufficient evidence. But track rules call for suspension of the owner and the trainer from racing while the investigation is going on. That could ruin both Worthington and Stinson financially.

"Then," Regan continued, "even if they're

cleared of the charges against them, the cloud of suspicion that hangs over them won't go away immediately. They won't get good odds on their horses; other owners will be afraid to bid on them in claiming races—in short, Worthington Farms would be out of business."

"That's awful!" Honey exclaimed indignantly.

"We have to get back to town before the race, to warn Mr. Stinson not to give Gadbox that feed bag," Trixie said desperately.

Just then, Trixie, Honey, and Regan were jostled again as the truck pulling their trailer made a sharp turn. Before they could recover, the truck stopped and the doors slammed. The three occupants of the trailer waited for further sounds. They heard the metallic noise of the trailer hitch being pulled loose. Then they heard the doors of the truck open and slam shut once again. The engine turned over and began running smoothly. Finally the noise of the truck receded.

The three sat in the dark stillness for a few moments, until they were sure that their captors had indeed left. Then Trixie whispered, "Honey, come over here and help me untie Regan."

"Why are you whispering?" Honey demanded in a normal tone. "And how can I help? My hands are tied behind my back, just as yours are."

"We'll have to work together," Trixie said out loud. "You're better with knots and things than I am, because of all your needlework. You be the hands, and I'll supply the eyes, as much as I can in this darkness."

Honey knelt on one side of Regan, her back turned so that her hands could reach the knots that bound his hands and feet. Trixie knelt facing him, directing Honey on which ropes to pull.

It was a long and frustrating process. Trixie, who could see what needed to be done, became impatient at Honey's groping clumsiness. Honey's arms grew stiff and sore from the awkward position she was forced to hold them in to work on the knots. Regan lay helplessly on his stomach, asking repeatedly if the girls were almost finished.

The heat and humidity became almost unbearable in the tight enclosure of the trailer. The only sound from outside was the chirping of crickets. Influenced by the stillness outside, the three people inside the trailer unconsciously lowered their voices once again to whispers.

After what seemed like hours, the last of the knots gave way, and Regan's arms and legs flopped free. Groaning, he pulled himself into a sitting position and massaged his wrists and flexed his ankles. Trixie and Honey waited impatiently, knowing that he couldn't untie them until some feeling returned to his own hands, but wishing that he would hurry. Finally he turned his attention to the two girls, and soon they, too, were massaging their wrists, rejoicing over their freedom.

"Why are we standing in here?" Trixie asked. "I want some fresh air!" She walked unsteadily to the back of the trailer and jumped out, falling to the ground as her still-numb legs gave way under her. Rolling over on her back, she raised her arms over her head and breathed in the clean, fresh air. Then, opening her eyes, she gasped, "It's daylight!"

The sun was, indeed, well over the eastern horizon. Honey, Trixie, and Regan exchanged panic-stricken glances. They were free—but where were they?

"We'll just have to start walking in some direction—any direction—and hope that we see a road sign that tells us where we are," Regan said.

"We were moving for a long time," Honey said hopelessly. "It could take us hours to get back to town on foot."

"Then we'll flag down a car," Trixie said, jumping to her feet and wincing as her stiff muscles protested. "The main thing is to get going. We have to get back to town before the race."

The tired threesome limped down the long driveway and out onto a gravel road. Trixie's muscles ached, she felt hot and dirty, and for the first time, she was noticing how hungry she was. Taking a deep breath, she resolved not to complain. *Honey and Regan are depressed enough already, without my making them feel worse*, she thought.

The gravel road eventually led to a two-lane blacktop, with a sign that said, "Saratoga, 10 miles." The three stared at the sign, and then Honey burst into tears, collapsing at the side of the road. "I—I can't walk ten more miles. I just can't!" she sobbed.

Completely dispirited, Trixie sat down beside Honey and put her arm around her friend. "I don't think I can, either. Regan?" she queried, looking up at the redheaded groom.

As if in answer, he sank down on the road beside them. "Sure, I can walk ten miles," he said. "But the way I feel right now, I'd need about three days to do it. Since we don't have three days, we might just as well wait right here and hope that someone comes by—someone trusting enough to pick up three dusty, dirty strangers on a deserted road miles from town, at about eight o'clock in the morning."

They sat and waited, but no cars went by. Finally, a dusty pickup truck came down the road, and the three stood up and waved frantically at it. The driver glanced at them, but he didn't slow down.

Trixie blinked back tears as she threw herself back down on the ground. *Nobody will stop,* she thought, *at least not in time.* "I don't even care if we save Gadbox anymore," she wailed. "I just want a shower, and some breakfast, and a long, long nap!"

Just then they heard the sound of a car coming down the road. "It's coming from the wrong direction," Honey said.

"That doesn't matter. If we get a ride somewhere, we can use a phone to call the track officials," Regan pointed out.

"They won't stop, anyway," Honey said, her spirits too low for her to try to think positively.

Trixie was staring intently at the station wagon that was approaching, and suddenly she was on her feet, dragging Honey up with her. "This car will stop, Honey!" she exclaimed. "I *know* it will!"

She began to jump up and down and wave her arms, and Honey, after a closer look at the car, began to wave and shout.

The car that skidded to a halt on the deserted road was the Bob-White station wagon, and as soon as it stopped, out piled Brian, Jim, Mart, and a big, burly young man with a pleasant, good-natured face.

"That's Johnny!" exclaimed Regan. "He's the guy who pawned my boots for me," he explained to the girls.

Danger at the Racetrack · 16

FOR THE NEXT several minutes, confusion reigned as everyone hugged and shouted at once. Finally, Mart Belden's piercing whistle split the air, startling the others into silence.

"The repatriation of our prodigal siblings is indeed an occasion that is cause for jubilation," he said. "But in order to terminate the anguish of a quartet of timorous elders, I suggest that we depart for Saratoga posthaste."

"Oh, Mart, have you talked to my parents?" Honey asked. "Are they terribly worried?"

"They certainly are," Jim answered before Mart could muster the large words he needed for a reply.

"They called your room early this morning. When there was no answer, they had the desk clerk let them in. Then they discovered that your beds hadn't been slept in, and they got frantic."

"Honey's parents called our parents," Brian continued, "and our parents called us at camp, thinking that we might know something about your whereabouts. We didn't, of course—in fact, we didn't even know you'd come to Saratoga, since you've obviously been too busy getting yourselves embroiled in a mystery to send us so much as a postcard."

Trixie looked at the ground and kicked a few roadside pebbles with her foot, too embarrassed to answer her brother.

"Listen," Jim interrupted, "I'm sure there's a very interesting story behind all this, and I want to hear all about it on the way into town. But I don't want to keep our folks waiting for us any longer than we have to."

"Gleeps!" Trixie exclaimed, suddenly remembering that race time was fast approaching. "We haven't a second to lose. Let's go!"

She ran to the car, with Honey and Regan close behind her, while the boys exchanged bewildered looks as they followed along.

On the way back to town, Trixie, Honey, and Regan quickly told the boys about the chain of events that had led up to that morning. "So you see," Trixie concluded, "we have to get back to town in time to warn Mr. Stinson not to give Gadbox the food that he prepared yesterday."

Jim nodded solemnly, his eyes on the road. "You also have to notify the track officials, so that they can try to catch those two crooks. They must be planning to bet on the race."

"Now you've heard our side of the story," Regan said, "but we still don't know how you came to find us on a deserted road ten miles from Saratoga—or how you and Johnny wound up together."

"Deductive perspicuity is not limited to the distaff side of the Bob-White conglomeration," Mart said smugly.

"Would somebody *else* tell the story, please," Trixie pleaded, "so that we can all understand it without using a dictionary, which doesn't happen to be standard equipment in the Bob-White station wagon?"

Brian chuckled. "Mart just means that we boys can follow clues as well as you girls can. When our folks called to say you'd disappeared in Saratoga, the three of us decided to skip the two-day counselors' party that ends the season, to drive down here and try to save your silly necks. When we got to the hotel a couple of hours ago, Mr. and Mrs. Wheeler had already questioned the desk clerk. He hadn't seen you leave, but he suggested that you might have gone riding again, since you had asked for a list of boarding stables in the area a couple of days ago. That didn't seem very logical, but since logic seldom has anything to do with your actions, we got the list of stables and started driving around to them."

"That's where they found me," Johnny said shyly. "I was worried about Regan, because he wasn't out working with the horses this morning, and he wasn't in the bunkhouse, either. Then the boys showed up, and they showed me Honey's and Trixie's class pictures, which they had in their billfoids."

"But you'd never seen the girls," Regan pointed out. "You weren't at the stable when they came out to see me."

"But you told me you'd had visitors," Johnny said. "Remember?" Regan nodded. "So I described how you look, and they all shouted, 'Regan!' Then I told them about how you'd come to the stable, and you didn't talk much about it, but I could tell you were real worried about something. Then I told them about how you were reading the paper a couple of nights ago in the bunkhouse, and about how you got real mad all of a sudden. When I asked why, you just said, 'Worthington's done it again!' and you wouldn't tell me anything more."

"I knew who Worthington was," Jim said, picking up the story, "because Dad had written to me at camp, saying that he was thinking of buying a horse from him. It was a flimsy lead, but it was all we had, so we took Johnny along with us and drove to the track."

"There we discovered that pandemonium had erupted due to the disappearance of two interlinked four-wheel vehicles," Mart put in.

"The pickup truck and horse trailer?" Trixie guessed.

"That's right," Brian told her. "One of the track employees had seen a pickup truck with a horse trailer going north out of town late last night. As long as we were following flimsy leads, we decided to head north to see if we could find any trace of those vehicles—or of you and Honey."

"That's when Johnny suggested that we check out that deserted farm," Jim added.

"Why *that* farm?" Trixie asked. "There must be dozens of deserted places around Saratoga."

"That used to be my farm," Johnny said softly. Seeing their surprised looks, he explained, "It was my father's, really. He raised horses there. Then he got real sick, and when he died, I had to sell the farm to pay the doctor's bills. The bank bought it, but they don't use it. It just sits there, all empty. Someday I want to buy it back. I think about that a lot. I—I guess that's why I thought about it when the boys asked me."

"It's lucky for us you did," Regan told his friend.

"It's been a lucky day for us all around," Trixie

said as the station wagon pulled up in front of the hotel. "I just hope our luck holds a little longer— until we contact Mr. Stinson, and until the track officials catch Scarface and his friend Louie."

Mr. and Mrs. Wheeler were both pacing the hotel lobby when the Bob-Whites, with Regan and Johnny, walked in. Mrs. Wheeler burst into tears and threw her arms around her daughter. Mr. Wheeler, blinking back tears of his own, forced himself to look angry. "I have a few things to say to you two," he said.

"Please, Mr. Wheeler, you'll have to wait," Trixie said, amazed at her own audacity. "I don't blame you for being angry, and as soon as this is all over, you can yell at us, or spank us, or make us stay in our rooms for a year. But right now, we have to save Gadbox."

Mr. Wheeler was too shocked to speak. He just stared in amazement as Jim Frayne reached into his pocket and pulled out a handful of change. "We'll use the pay phones here in the lobby," he said, handing coins to the other Bob-Whites. "Brian, you call your parents, collect, and tell them that Trixie's all right. Trix, call Mr. Stinson and stop him from feeding Gadbox. Mart, call the track officials and tell them about Scarface and Louie. And please, try to limit your vocabulary to words that mere grown-ups can understand. Honey, you and Regan and I will stay here and try to explain this mixed-up mess to our parents.''

A few minutes later, Trixie returned to the couches in the lobby, where the Wheelers were sitting with Regan, Jim, Honey, and Johnny. "I got through to Mr. Stinson," she crowed. "He hadn't fed Gadbox yet, and he's not going to—I mean, he's not going to feed him the drugged feed in the feed bag. It took me a little while to convince him that I knew what I was talking about, but finally he believed me."

"I'm not sure that I believe any of this," Mr. Wheeler said. "I'm beginning to understand how the sequence of events fits together, but I still don't understand how you girls managed to be hot on the trail of a mystery, right under my nose, without my being aware of it."

"We'll explain all that later," Trixie assured him.

"You certainly will," Brian said as he walked up behind her. "I just finished talking to Dad and Moms, and although they're relieved to find out that your sandy head is still on your shoulders, I'd say you'll have a lot of explaining to do when you get back to Sleepyside."

"Oh, woe," Trixie groaned. "Even after I finish explaining things, they'll probably make sure that I don't leave my room until school starts in September."

Trixie's worries about her fate were interrupted by Mart, who returned from talking to the track officials. "I told them the whole story in words of one syllable," he said. "They thought it was a crank call, but right in the middle of the conversation, Carl Stinson walked into their office with the feed bag and asked them to have it tested for drugs. That got their attention, all right." He chuckled. "Anyway, they want Honey and Trixie to talk to the police."

"Don't tell me we have to go to the police station right now!" Trixie protested. "I want to do everything I can to make sure that Scarface and Louie are put behind bars, where they belong. But if I don't get something to eat, I'll faint dead away."

Mart nodded. "Never let it be said that I am not cognizant of alimentary considerations," he said, grinning. "The police are going to meet us at the hotel coffee shop in fifteen minutes."

"Yippee!" Trixie shouted, leaping up from the couch. "Let's eat!"

Between bites of their food, the Bob-Whites, with help from Regan and Johnny, once again told their story, this time to two plainclothes police officers. The officers listened intently, nodding from time to time and taking occasional notes.

"Then as far as you know," Officer Ryan concluded, "these two men, whom you call 'Scarface' and 'Louie,' have no way of knowing that you three have escaped and warned Mr. Stinson."

Trixie shook her head. "I don't see how they *could* know," she said.

"In that case," Officer Johnson said solemnly, "we'll have to ask you girls to do us a favor—unless, of course, you absolutely refuse to work *with* the police."

Trixie and Honey blushed and exchanged guilty looks. "We—We'll do whatever you say," Trixie said humbly.

"Wait until you hear what we're asking of you before you agree," Officer Ryan cautioned. "There is a small element of danger involved. We'd like you to go to the track this afternoon, where we'll position you somewhere near the betting windows. If you see Scarface or Louie placing a bet, you'll give us a signal. Then we'll come forward and arrest them."

"Couldn't I do it?" Regan asked. "I hate to see Honey and Trixie taking any more risks."

Officer Johnson shook his head. "With your red hair, you'd stand out like a warning flag. Scarface and Louie wouldn't get within a block of that betting window. Besides, while I can't say that there's no risk involved, I *can* say that we'll be nearby, ready to intervene as soon as Honey or Trixie gives the signal."

"We'll be all right, Regan," Trixie assured her friend. "After all we've gone through so far because of Scarface and Louie, I'd be downright upset if we didn't have a hand in their arrest. Right, Honey?"

Honey nodded. "A few minutes ago, I'd have said I couldn't even stay awake until race time. But the food has picked me up, and if you'll just give us a few minutes to shower and change clothes, we'll be ready to go."

Less than an hour later, Trixie and Honey were in their assigned places at a concession stand across from the betting windows. Each girl was holding a hot dog in one hand and a soft drink in the other, and they'd been instructed to eat and drink slowly, so that casual passersby would think they were just having a snack before returning to the stands. "If you see either of the suspects," Officer Johnson had told them, "don't act excited. Just throw the remainder of your hot dog into this trash can. That will be our signal to come forward."

The girls stood quiet, their eyes searching the crowd for a sign of the two culprits. The claiming race was announced over the loudspeaker as the next event, and still the two men had not appeared. *They only have a couple of minutes left to put their bets down*, Trixie thought. *What if they somehow found out that we escaped and tipped off Mr. Stinson? What if they don't show up?*

The line at the ticket windows began to dwindle as the field of horses for the claiming race was led onto the track. The crowd of people who had been

placing bets or buying refreshments surged forward to take their places in the stands.

Suddenly Trixie spotted Scarface approaching
the ticket window. She looked at Honey, and the
two girls tossed their hot dogs into the trash can;
they waited breathlessly. Ten seconds went by,
then fifteen, and still the two officers had not come
forward to make their arrest.

With the lines of bettors gone, it took Scarface
less than a minute to buy his tickets and turn from
the window. "He'll get away, Honey!" Trixie said
desperately. Unthinkingly, she ran toward him.
"Somebody stop that man!" she shouted.

Scarface whirled to face her, drawing a gun from
his jacket pocket as he turned. A look of surprise
crossed his face as he recognized Trixie. "You
again!" he snarled. He raised the gun and leveled it
at Trixie. Before he had time to pull the trigger,
Regan, emerging from nowhere, forced him to the
ground.

Officers Ryan and Johnson came out of the
crowd seconds later and hauled Scarface to his feet,
fastening a pair of handcuffs around his wrists.

"Are you all right?" Officer Ryan demanded.

Trixie gulped and nodded, suddenly weak-kneed.

"We saw your signal," Officer Johnson explained,
"but we got trapped in the crowd of people going
back to their seats before the race. We couldn't get
through."

"I'm just glad Regan did," Trixie said gratefully. "Otherwise, I'd be—" Her voice failed her, and she gulped.

"Attempted murder—that's one more charge we'll book you on," Officer Ryan told Scarface. "Come on, we're going downtown."

"Wait!" Trixie ordered as a cheer erupted from the stands. "Everybody be quiet!"

Straining their ears to hear above the cheering of the crowd, the girls and Regan, along with the two officers and Scarface, heard the announcer's voice over the loudspeakers: "And the winner, by five lengths, is Gadbox!"

A Celebration Party • 17

THAT EVENING, Trixie and Honey, refreshed after a long nap and dressed in the best outfits they'd brought to Saratoga, entered the hotel dining room. The hostess escorted them to the largest table in the room, where the rest of their party had already gathered for a celebration dinner.

Jim Frayne held Trixie's chair as she sat down, then took his seat next to her. Brian did the same for Honey. Looking around the table, Trixie smiled in turn at Mr. Worthington, Mr. Stinson, Mr. and Mrs. Wheeler, and Mart. Her smile turned into a wide, delighted grin as her eyes landed on Regan and Joan Stinson, sitting side by side across from her. Regan's friend Johnny, looking uncomfortable in a suit and tie, was sitting on the other side of Joan.

As soon as the girls were seated, Mr. Worthington signaled their waiter, and he came to the table bearing a tray on which rested twelve champagne glasses, each one filled with bubbling liquid.

Trixie stared at the glass that was set before her, then looked apologetically at Mr. Worthington. "I can't—" she began.

"Yes, you can," Jim whispered into her ear. "Our glasses are filled with ginger ale."

Trixie giggled and lifted her glass. "In that case ..." she said, looking expectantly at Mr. Worthington, who had risen to his feet to propose a toast.

"To Honey and Trixie," he said, "who saved Worthington Farms from disaster."

"And to Brian, Mart, Jim, Regan, and Johnny, who saved Honey and Trixie from disaster," Mr. Wheeler added.

Trixie and Honey ducked their heads in embarrassment, then joined in the general laughter.

"You'll all be happy to know," Mr. Worthington said as he sat back down, "that I had a call from Officer Ryan before I came here tonight. He says that Scarface has confessed that he drugged Gadfly seven years ago and attempted to drug Gadbox yesterday."

"What about Louie?" Honey asked. "Did he get away?"

Mr. Worthington shook his head. "The saying that there's honor among thieves is a great exaggeration," he said. "As soon as Scarface realized that he was going to be in prison for a good long while, he was only too happy to assure himself of some company. He told the police exactly where to find his accomplice, who is now also behind bars. And Louie, not to be outdone as a traitor, told the police about four other instances in which he and his former friend had pulled the same trick at other tracks around the country."

"It's all my fault," Carl Stinson blurted suddenly. The others at the table all looked at him in surprise. "That man with the scar talked to me seven years ago. Offered me a lot of money if I'd slip Gadfly some drugs before the race. Explained the whole deal—how they'd wait for a race where there was one heavy favorite, and another sure thing for second place. Then they'd do something to make sure number one was disqualified, and bet heavily on number two at tremendous odds.

"I turned him down flat, of course," Stinson continued. "I should have turned him *in*. But he threatened Joan's life if I told the police, so I kept my mouth shut. It never occurred to me that he'd sneak into the track in the dead of night and find Gadfly's feed bag. I always kept it so well hidden."

"I was the only other person who knew where the feed was kept, so of course you suspected me," Regan said, understandingly.

Stinson nodded. "That's not all. When I told Scarface I wasn't interested in his offer, he told me he'd go to you. I laughed in his face. 'Regan wouldn't turn against me,' I said. But then, when the drugs were discovered, I just assumed—I'm sorry. I should have had more faith in you, Regan."

"My running away wasn't a move that would inspire faith, Carl. Anyway, that's all in the past. Now it's time to think about the future."

Trixie thought she saw Regan glance at Joan Stinson as he said "the future."

"That's right," J. T. Worthington said heartily. "We can't relive the past, but we *can* do what we can to make up for past mistakes. I've made quite a few mistakes, but I'm ready to try to make up for them. Carl told me this afternoon that the scarfaced man had approached him seven years ago. I was impressed at the loyalty he showed to me—and to Gadfly—in turning down that offer. After he left, I started thinking, and I realized that I haven't shown the same kind of loyalty to him. I put my own interests first on two separate occasions, when financial setbacks caused me to enter in claiming races the best horses Carl ever had."

"Gleeps!" Trixie shouted, then clapped her hand over her mouth as she realized that shouting was not in keeping with the elegance of the restaurant. "I forgot, in my excitement over Gadbox's winning the race and not being disqualified, that it was a *claiming* race. Did someone claim him?"

Mr. Worthington nodded solemnly. "Someone did, indeed. But I found the new owner and bought Gadbox back." Reaching into his breast pocket, Worthington brought out two pieces of paper. He handed them to Carl Stinson. "Here are the papers for Gadbox and Gadfly. You've been a fine trainer, Carl. Now it's your chance for you to prove yourself as an owner."

Carl Stinson stared at the pieces of paper in his hand, then looked at Worthington. Finally, the reality of what had just happened dawned on him, and he let out a whoop of joy that caused the other diners in the restaurant to turn and stare. Unmindful of the attention he was getting, Stinson turned to Regan and slapped him on the back. "Did you hear that?" he demanded. "We're in business!"

Regan smiled. "I'm happy for you, Carl. But I can't come to work for you. I have a home now in Sleepyside, and I want to go back. That is," he added, looking at Mr. Wheeler, "if I still have a job to go back to."

"You know you do, Regan," Mr. Wheeler said.

Regan acknowledged Mr. Wheeler's quiet reassurance with a smile. Then, turning back to Carl Stinson, he said, "You know, if you need a good hand with horses, I'd be happy to introduce you to one of the best. He's sitting right at this table."

Johnny looked around the table to see whom Regan was referring to, then flushed as he saw everyone staring back at him.

"I think, too," Regan continued, "that Johnny could recommend a good piece of property where you could set up Stinson Farms. Right, Johnny?"

"Right!" Johnny exclaimed boldly. "I'm sure the bank would sell us my dad's place real cheap, Mr. Stinson. *They* aren't using it."

"We'll drive out to look at it tomorrow," Carl promised, "right after we sit down and discuss your wages. But I wish you'd reconsider, Regan," he added, turning back to the redheaded groom. "I hate to lose you again."

"You won't lose me entirely," Regan said. "I plan to be around a lot." This time there was no mistaking the look he directed at Joan Stinson, a look she returned with a smile.

"Isn't it all perfectly perfect?" Honey asked as she and Trixie both lay in bed that night, staring at the ceiling and reviewing the day's sometimes exciting, sometimes frightening events.

"No, it isn't," Trixie said. "It won't be perfectly perfect until the Bob-Whites run two small errands tomorrow morning, just before we all go home to Sleepyside."

"Two small errands? What are they?" Honey asked.

Trixie told her, and when Honey fell asleep, moments later, she was still smiling.

The next morning, Matthew Wheeler was once again pacing the lobby impatiently. Mrs. Wheeler sat on a couch nearby, twisting her handkerchief. A short distance away, Regan and Joan Stinson stood talking quietly, saying their good-byes and making plans to see each other again.

"Where are those children?" Mr. Wheeler exploded. "First Honey and Trixie disappear, then the boys find them and bring them back, then they all disappear again! I thought Jim had some small measure of common sense. How could he let this happen?"

"Calm down, dear," Mrs. Wheeler said, trying to hide her nervousness. "I'm sure the children will all be back any second."

As if on cue, the Bob-White station wagon pulled up in front of the hotel, and the five laughing, excited teen-agers piled out and ran into the lobby. Trixie was carrying a large white box in her hands, and Honey had another, smaller box of the same color and shape.

"Where have you been?" Mr. Wheeler roared. "We're ready to leave."

"So are we, Daddy," Honey said. "But we

couldn't leave while Regan and Bobby were still missing."

"Regan isn't missing," Mr. Wheeler said. "He's right here."

"And what's this about Bobby?" Regan demanded.

The Bob-Whites exchanged conspiratorial glances. "First of all, Regan," Trixie began, "you *are* still missing. You're missing these." Taking the top off the box she was holding, Trixie revealed its contents: Regan's treasured riding boots.

"And," Honey continued before anyone could speak, "since Bobby has been missing all of us since we've been away, and we promised to bring him a souvenir, we got him these." She opened the smaller box she was holding. Inside was a pair of child-sized riding boots. "Of course, they aren't handmade and monogrammed, like yours, but we're sure Bobby will love them."

"I'm sure he will, too," Mr. Wheeler said, his anger completely vanished.

"I can't wait to see the look on his face," Jim said.

"Then let's not wait another minute!" Trixie exclaimed. "All aboard the Bob-White express! Next stop: Sleepyside-on-the-Hudson!"

The Bob-Whites, plus Regan, all piled into the station wagon. Mr. and Mrs. Wheeler got into their waiting car. As the two cars pulled away, Joan Stinson, looking sad and happy at the same time, stood at the curb. Regan, leaning out the window, continued to wave to her until the station wagon turned a corner and she was lost from sight.

Sitting in the front seat next to Jim, Trixie stared, unseeing, at the road ahead. *Regan has a girl friend, Carl Stinson has two horses, Johnny has a good job, and Bobby has a pair of riding boots*, she thought happily.

Catching sight of Trixie's beaming face in the rearview mirror, Jim said, "I don't know how you can look so pleased with yourself, Trixie, when you've been in and out of danger so many times in the past few days."

"And when you're going to be in danger of a stern lecture when we get home," Brian added.

"*And* when a rudimentary perusal of past predicaments predicates similar situations in the ensuing seasons," Mart concluded.

"I know, I know," Trixie said. "I've been in danger in the past, and I will be again in the future, more than likely. But right this minute—" She glanced at Honey, who read her thoughts.

"Everything's perfectly perfect!" the two girls said together.

Amid a chorus of laughter, the Bob-Whites settled back for the ride home.